COLD HEARTED

a novel by

NAGHILIA DESRAVINES

This book is a fiction. Names, Characters, places, and incidents either are products of the author's imagination or are used fictitiously. Any resemblance to actual events or locales or person, living or dead, is entirely coincidental.

Copyright © 2014 by **Naghilia Desravines**

First published in United States of America in 2014
By Naghilia Publishing
www.naghiliadesravines.com

Naghilia Desravines has asserted her right under the Copyright, Designs, and Patents Act 1988, to be identified as the author of this work.

All rights reserved, no part of this publication may be reproduced or transmitted or utilized in any form or by any means, electronic, mechanical, photocopying or otherwise, without the prior permission from the publisher.

Cover design and interior design by
Wonderbug Creations
Cover photo by Adept Studios

Printed and Bound in Unites States of America

Paperback ISBN: 978-0-9904531-0-9
E-book ISBN: 978-0-9904531-1-6

LCCN: 2014912201

For My Son Shem,

With All My Love and Gratitude

Acknowledgments

I acknowledge, with gratitude, all the people who saw me through this book and supported this endeavor during the difficult times. I extend my sincere thanks to my family, friends, Anthony Echo, Sharlene Belice, Perry Wilson, Amy G, Kenji Kita, Iliyana Omereva, and Nicole Williams, for all your aid and foresight.

"You can't connect the dots looking forward; you can only connect them looking backwards. So you have to trust that the dots will somehow connect in your future. You have to trust in something: your gut, destiny, life, karma, whatever. This approach has never let me down, and it has made all the difference in my life".

Steve Jobs

PROLOGUE

Late evening, a residential street in Whitney, Las Vegas.

"No! We need to stop."
"That's all, everybody. We've done our best. Wrap it up here!"

Cáel opened her eyes. The sky was a dark blanket looming above. She could sense flashing red and slowly perceived ambulances, police cruisers, fire trucks, chaos. She shut her eyes.

Very carefully, she opened them again. There was rapid movement around her. She turned her head gradually; every move was an excruciating exercise in physical pain. A smear of yellow caught her vision. Yellow crime-scene tape, her brain groggily acknowledged. There was a face a meter from her and a meter's grasp in her memory. Very thin mouth; she knew that mouth well, but for some reason, she could not give a name to it. Chinese eyes, round face, but his eyes were closed.

A low, droning sound buzzed from his feet, up his legs, past his waist, and to his shoulders. The hand tugging on the zip paused for a second, and then finished the job, closing the bag up tightly.

"A sleeping bag," Cáel registered inwardly, "they've put him in a sleeping bag, because he's sleeping. Oh no! There's no gap, they've sealed him in! How is he going to breathe? Help! You'll kill him!" She wanted to shout, alarmed, but her voice strangled in her throat and ended there.

"Oh shit, they'll do it to me next," she thought. "I'm not asleep, I'm awake!"

Panic rose from inside her, willing her to move, but she couldn't shake a muscle in her body. She could hear a scream in her head, a frenzied yell, but her lips would not move.

Someone grabbed her legs, and then someone else took her arms. An overwhelming feeling of resignation engulfed her.

This is it, and it's my turn. They're going to put me in a bag. They're going to zip me and seal me in.

Cáel felt the hard, unyielding stretch of a board under her back, her limbs deadweight. The heady tickle of being lifted off the ground… into a van.

"I'm in a vehicle," she tried to clear her thoughts. "Oh, thank God, they didn't zip me in! The door is closing. Are we leaving him behind?"

Unhinged thoughts invaded Cáel's weak consciousness, swimming in and out of sync with one another. She heard the door open.

"Oh, the door's open again. That'll be him now," she guessed. "Maybe I can ask them to unzip him a bit so I can see his face, and he can get some air... Oh! It's not him."

Cáel tried to place the face in front of her. She wanted to ask who it was, this man who staring at her, his manic eyes fixed on her face. But she couldn't speak. She vaguely noticed the man's eyes were not the same color as dizziness assailed her and she slowly drifted into a sweet black hole of unconscious surrender — Coma.

CHAPTER 1

Two weeks later, in a private recovery room at the University Medical Center in Las Vegas, the yellow curtains were opened and an afternoon light sat gently in the room. Cáel stood by the window. It had been her friend, allowing her look out, keeping the universe away — the tranquility of a fishbowl when the fish weren't moving. She'd been standing there for the last half hour, looking to the outside but registering only a blank. She gazed at the low mountains far away. They were bare and brown. No layers, no depth, like new buildings, and new clothes, and new lovers. Like her. Waiting for time and history to etch them and tell them their worth.

"You're all set? Your discharge papers are ready for signatures."

Cáel turned around from the window to face the nurse who had just breezed in. "Your friend will be here soon to pick you up," the nurse said, flipping through the papers in her hand. "You remember Amanda Erikson, don't you? She was here last week. She got you that lovely bunch of red roses there, Cáel, your favorite flowers. They were so lovely!"

The nurse rattled on cheerfully for a few moments, then furrowed her brow in concern. "Now, remember what the doctor's instructed, Cáel. You've been out of coma just ten days. You need to recuperate and give yourself enough rest. Your memory will hopefully come back as the swelling in your brain recedes, but under no circumstances should you stress yourself in any way, it's not good for the baby."

The baby, Cáel contemplated inside her head, and gave a long look to the kind nurse. Jocelyn, the Philippine medical worker, was the only person she had any real human relationship with. Everyone else she'd met since she'd awakened from the coma were simply names, and, faces owning those names, who were supposed to mean something to her. Her memory had deserted her completely, and the visitors had only disconcerted her and left her raw.

Cáel went back to looking out the window. She caught a hint of her own reflection in the glass and vaguely recognized the face that stared back at her — Cáel Darcie's face — brown, perky, bandaged, and damaged. She knew it was a face she'd studied a million times, it was, after all, her own. That's just about all she knew about her face that morning. She quickly turned away.

Her sister, Myra, reached a day after she had gained consciousness, had been next to her most daylight hours. Cáel had been groggy and sleeping most of that time, but whenever she had awakened, she'd find her younger sister's quiet presence in the room — curled up in a chair reading a thick book. Cáel didn't know the title, but she sensed Myra was only using it as a distraction, something to pass the time.

Myra was a carbon copy of Cáel in appearance as well as temperament. Just out of college, Myra worked as a company secretary and lived with their mother. Cáel was Myra's heroine, just as her oldest sister, Sarah, was Cáel's.

She didn't remember anything since she'd been conscious, and Myra gave her space. Cáel never asked her a question, and Myra never questioned her, other than how she was feeling. But she jumped out of the chair to help her or to pass her water or medicines whenever there was requirement, and she accompanied her to all her tests and checks, a worried expression permanently scrolled on her face.

The woman who claimed to be Cáel's best friend opened the door and walked in, jolting her into the real world. Amanda Erikson was blond, petite, and bohemian. An unhinged scene of a younger version of Amanda and herself flashed through Cáel's mind — they were walking in a crowded street, jostling in the madness, reveling in youth, laughing and joking, sharing a food-carton full of chicken noodles. Oh, there was one more scene. A nightclub, beer and cocktails being passed around, chatter, music... Cáel just had the name of the song... its coming... coming...Yes. Red Lipstick, Rihanna.

The scenes came and went. Cáel could almost smell the cigarette-lit air of that nightclub, so strong was the recollection. This was her first recollection since she'd awakened. She gazed at Amanda, unsure, taking in her light-green flowery short dress, her big yellow tote bag, and carelessly fixed hair. Amanda gazed right back, her kohl-lined eyes worried, moist.

Behind Amanda, Myra entered with a duffel bag on her shoulder. She was dressed in tight slacks and a light cotton shirt. She approached Cáel and gave her a long hug. Worry marked her brows as she studied her face.

"I got a bag. Let me pack your stuff," Amanda said. "Let's go home, babe."
What was home and where was it? Cáel wondered but said nothing.

***

"Pull your seatbelt on, Cáel," Amanda said, reversing the car out of the parking lot slowly. The smell in the car caught in the back of Cáel's throat. It smelled in there, like blood, dirt, and vomit all mixed up. She felt sick. She tried to picture what Amanda's home looked like.

Am I heading to her house?
She didn't want to go there. She felt an overwhelming urge to run back to the safety of the hospital, where everyone was kind to her. Cáel stole a glance at Amanda. With her eyes trained on the road, Amanda was frowning, her lips clamped shut, locked together in a grim, thin line.
I'll go back, shall I? Shall I do it? Yank the handle and kick the door open? Jump out and

start running? Too late, Cáel reflected, as Amanda turned the corner and accelerated. The sturdy, lumbering structure of University Medical Center was gone.

She felt trapped.

"Cáel, hold the seatbelt loose around your tummy," Myra advised her from the back. Cáel glanced at her, she had forgotten her totally. A memory of her younger sister went racing through her head. In the memory, they were quarrelling about who was going to get which bed in their bedroom.

Cáel pressed her forehead against the window. She was connected with it, her protection. The glass was cold against her cheek. The city whizzed by, a burst of buildings and people, a confusing blur to her. The roads and the many places on those roads looked so familiar, yet so alien. She wished this could all go away, she hated the confusion. As the car braked for a stop sign, Cáel shook her head, trying to shake away the perplexity and the tears that were threatening to spill and drown her. She heard a voice in her head saying over and over, "Stop! You won't get away with this!" It was her voice. She blinked hard and bit her lip to fight back the nausea welling inside her stomach.

An old woman was pushing a shopping cart past the stop sign. She wore slippers, her feet grimy. Cáel caved in to the nausea, opening the door, rolling out, and vomiting everything inside her. The next second, the road was a bilious smear and she was on her haunches, stupefied. The old woman walked over to her and gave her a bottle of water. She felt Myra next to her as she cleaned her mouth and face.

Amanda held the car door open for Cáel, who crawled back in, doubling up in numbness. The car moved and Cáel pressed harder against the glass, spit drooling from her lips which were spread like two slugs.

Suddenly panic gripped her. She felt a tug in her womb, and it tightened and tightened until she was a taut ball of fat and muscle and tissue. She felt bloated and she needed to vomit it all out. The nausea had to go away before it consumed her completely. She thrashed about in her seat, claustrophobic, yanking at the seatbelt.

Amanda gawked at her with red-rimmed eyes. Then reaching across the gap, she tugged at Cáel's arms. Cáel resisted.
"What are you doing?" Amanda squealed. "Don't you think you've done enough damage already? Stop being an idiot!"

Instantly, echoes of all the other times Cáel had got called an idiot by someone invaded her head, stretching back through time like a hall of mirrors. She retreated to the other side of the car, tears running down her face.

I know it's true what they've all been saying, she told herself. She is my best friend and my my only friend.

She felt her stomach falling down inside her as broken memories cartwheeled through her mind. Amanda's scraped back, the sting of her hand, raised voices, a man shouting, a woman screaming, doors slamming. Other memories too, a whole plethora of them she couldn't get hold of yet. But one thing was certain — Amanda was her best friend. She was still not sure if she loved her or hated her, if she was scared of her, or felt sorry for her, but she knew Amanda was the only friend she had at that point in her lost life.

CHAPTER 2

"Look, I know you've been through a lot. You've been in coma," Amanda said, while aggressively maneuvering through traffic. "You can't remember zilch of your life and you're pregnant."

Cáel turned sharply to Amanda.

"I know it's a lot to handle for a twenty-seven year old, but you've got to keep it together, all right?" Amanda continued.

Cáel scrubbed away her tears. Oh, how old am I? I don't even know that, she thought. Twenty-seven years old, for god's sake! Pregnant. She desperately tried to hold onto her sanity and keep in the vomit. She fought the urge to run back to the hospital.

The world seemed scary right now, and Cáel tried not to panic again. She went back to looking out, trying to divert her consciousness away from the nausea. Everything looked so normal. There were shops and big buildings and cars and people all over. She recognized some of it and none of it. Her thoughts were fragmented, muddled. They had driven past many signs that said 'Welcome to Las Vegas.' So they must be in Las Vegas, probably downtown, or the strip, Cáel concluded.

Her brain gradually started to remember facts and specifics about Vegas. Words and pictures popped rapidly in her brain — Las Vegas, the sin city, and neon glitter-gulch. The twenty-five-foot tall sign located on Las Vegas Boulevard South saying, 'Welcome to fabulous Las Vegas, Nevada'— the sign that marked the classic start to the famous Las Vegas Strip burned and singed her mind.

The famous saying, what was that? Cáel asked herself. *What happens in Vegas, stays in Vegas*, she recollected. She closed her eyes, concentrating, not wanting to let go of the vivid details crashing through the roadblocks in her memory channels. She remembered the fountains, dancing and swaying as though alive. *Bellagio, yes, she thought, that is the name, it's a casino, and it's called Bellagio. I've seen a movie about it as well, she told herself. The fountains are timed to music, a Michael Jackson song — Billie Jean, they swayed the Jackson way.*

She opened her eyes. They appeared to be heading into a residential area. A sign informed her they were in West Henderson. Cáel took in the wide open, clean streets, held together by spacious walk paths running on either side. The landscape was flat, dotted with palms and shrubs. She had an instant vision of sand and dust, and bright sun.

"Mojave Desert, Nevada," she muttered to herself, feeling a little more oriented than she was when she'd left the hospital.

Amanda headed into smaller street, passing a few apartment complexes. "Nearly there,"

Amanda said as they turned into another street. "We all felt it would be better if you stay with me for a few days until you feel better, and you're able to drive around. It's difficult for me to stay at your place with you because of work in my own."

"I feel I should stay at my own place. Myra can stay with me," Cáel said with uncertainty. She wanted to be in her own home, with familiar things, so that she could revive her memory bit by bit.

"I can't stay longer, Cáel, though I really wish I could. I've been here for over a week, I have to get back to work but you can come with me," Myra answered.

Come where? Where are you going? Cáel wanted to ask, wanting to remember, but felt too lost to think more. She didn't say anything.

Their car came to a halt in front of a quaint four-story apartment building. A little plaque on a stick embedded in the tiny landscaped lawn informed 'Corel Apartments, Harris Street.' Amanda soon parked and they got out. "Third-floor, let's take the elevator, you're not well enough for stairs, mommy-to-be."

She said it like it's rendered me worthless, Cáel thought. *Thanks, but I can do without the name-calling, you "best-friend" to mommy-to-be.* Cáel was suddenly taken aback by her sarcasm, and gingerly followed Amanda into her home. Myra carried Cáel's bag and medicines behind them.

It smelled like last night's ashtray. The tiny foyer opened into a living room furnished with a bright red couch, a couple of leather bean-bags, and a beautiful white fluffy rug on the floor-tiles. A huge painting of red poppies hung on a purple wall. A television graced the facing wall. Little knick-knacks of tribal origins filled the square wooden coffee table in the center of the living room. The only other piece of furniture was a huge teak-wood shelf, filled with hundreds of books and photo-frames.

Cáel crept closer to the photographs. There were many pictures of her and Amanda. She picked one and peered at it. As she held the frame, a flashback of that day popped in her head. She looked at Amanda, who was still standing in the foyer, handbag on her shoulder, hands clutching the straps, studying Cáel, her eyes dark smears of kohl.

"What happened to your hair?" Cáel asked.

"Nothing. I colored it, remember? You said you loved it. You said blonde worked for me," replied Amanda, smiling. She moved, finally, breezing into the living room and dropped her heavy bag on the couch with a plop. Then she looked at Cáel and Myra, her hands akimbo.

"You really don't remember anything, do you? Gosh, all this is so crazy!" Myra said, facing Cáel. This was the first time the placid Myra had strongly commented on anything, and Cáel was rather taken aback.

Amanda waved her hands in the air and then ran them through her long hair. "Okay, first things first! Let me give you some clothes, you go shower, and I'll fix you something to eat. Myra, help."

Oh great, thanks! First things first, Cáel repeated in her head.

Amanda went on, "Something healthy for the baby, the doctor — Dr. Davis, he gave me a list of nutrition for you and the little angel." Amanda approached Cáel and touched her belly, "Hello, little one, Aunt Amanda here!"

Cáel pulled back. "Please, stop that, it's embarrassing."

Amanda straightened up, frowned, and walked past her. Cáel followed Amanda through a small corridor, into a decent-sized room — Amanda's bedroom. There was a queen-size bed with women's clothes strewn over it. Goblets, colored bottles and creams, and all sorts of makeup littered the top of a scruffy chest of drawers. A sense of great acquaintance ran through Cáel and she knew she had been in this room countless times. A large mirror was nailed to the wall above the chest. It was framed in a thick golden frame, chubby cupids held it up.

Cáel avoided looking in the mirror. She realized she had been careful not to catch a glimpse of herself, avoiding mirrors and reflecting windows all afternoon, afraid to face what she saw every time she did.

She ran the shower and stood motionless, letting the hot steamy water drench her. Her thoughts traveled back to the guy in the bag and the other one in the ambulance. They must be friends. Friends of mine? Must be. If not, why were all three of us at the same location? The pictures in her head were like cobwebs strung across dim doorways. Fragile. She didn't want to walk through and break them. She didn't want them to go. She just wanted to stand there and watch until it all made sense. She felt the sting of small jets of heated water on her back. Nothing was slotting into place. Her recollections were disjointed, fragments, and she needed a thread to weave them all together. Right now they were like a word on the tip of her tongue — there but not quite there. If only she could just stand and watch...

Loud banging on the door broke her reverie.

"Are you done, Cáel? The food is getting cold!"

It was Myra.

"Yes, five minutes!"

"Come on. I need a drink."

Cáel turned the shower knob and stepped out. Her entire being was aware of the huge mirror that covered one entire wall of the bath.

She had tried not to acknowledge it on her way in. But she knew she couldn't put it off any longer. She couldn't evade reality. That, or the baby.

  Slowly, ever so slowly, Cáel turned and faced the mirror. A beautiful black woman stared back at her. Jet-black long curly hair framed that beautiful face, with determined, defiant brown eyes and a soft, almost gullible mouth.

"This is who I am," Cáel told herself.

Who was she?

  Her body was not tall, not short, but svelte, broad-shouldered, full-bosomed, full-hipped, with toned, capable arms. Tentatively, her hands felt her stomach. It was yielding, not yet rounded with a growing baby.

  Cáel glared deep into her own eyes, and felt a resolve stir her. It was an old feeling, for she had been a determined and ambitious person most of her life, though she didn't know it just now. She promised that woman in the mirror that she would rediscover her and uncover everything else that had been. The resolve traveled through her heart and into her womb. And it was then that she knew how dear that oblivious life living inside her was to her. She knew she had wanted that little being in her world, more than anything else. An image of the dead man in the zip-bag assaulted her right then. They were connected, her baby and that man. She just didn't know it yet how they connected together.

Cáel pursed her lips in grim determination, silently wording a promise to herself and her unborn child. Wrapping a towel around her bare body, she went out, ready to face it all.

CHAPTER 3

"Finally! What took you so long?" Myra rolled her eyes and smiled at her older sister as she entered, looking fresh and lucid.

Amanda was toasting bread slices in a tiny toaster. Her kitchen was small, and it appeared to be bursting at the seams with clutter. A little table stood along the one free wall, next to a lace-curtained window. Four straight-backed chairs gave it company. Hot steaming pasta in white sauce sat mutely between the plates on the table, filling the kitchen with an inviting aroma. Cáel leaned against the kitchen sliding door, now dressed in a blue denim skirt and a mauve racerback. She felt light and rational after her bath and after her resolve.

A memory came back as she took in the ambiance. Cáel and Amanda were at the same table, eating with other people.

There was a lot of chatter going around.

A memory from happier times, she guessed, and half smiled.

"You just remembered something, didn't you?" Amanda asked, seeing her smile.

"No, nothing," replied Cáel, pulling herself a chair, "nothing substantial anyway, I mean. I keep getting these flashes and images, but nothing that's making sense."

"Well, don't worry. The doc said your memory will come back with time," Myra reassured her, sitting herself down across from Cáel.

"I hope so, I feel lost."

"C'mon babe, don't. You're with people who love you! You'll be fine. You're already looking better," Amanda chipped in, sitting down herself and spooning in some pasta on the plates.

"I just called Mum to let her know you're at

Amanda's," Myra informed Cáel. "They've been worried sick about you. Maybe you should talk to Mum. She was here for a few days while you were unconscious. When she went back, I came."

They. My family. Yeah, as soon as I remember their names or numbers, I shall call them, she thought. There was suddenly a lump in her throat. She swallowed hard, forcing the food down.

"Sorry, you want something to drink? I've got orange juice, I think." Amanda got up and pulled open the fridge door. Soon she was back at the table with a glass of orange juice and a bottle of wine. She poured a glass for Myra.

"Your mom and older sis came to meet you right after you woke up. You remember?"

Amanda asked, downing a full glass of wine in one go.

"Yeah, vaguely, I was groggy. Umm, where do they live? Where do I live?"

Cáel addressed the latter half of the question to Myra, and then looked from Myra to Amanda, back to Myra. She noticed Myra's eyes were filling up with tears. She opened her mouth to speak and then shut it, changing her mind.

"Your mom's in Fort Lauderdale, girl," Amanda replied. "You live in a condo in Black Mountain. It's close by, and it's your own condo. You bought it a few months ago, and you were thrilled!"

Recollections came rushing by. An automatic garage door opening, Amanda besides her in the car. Her car? A keychain with a glittering mermaid hanging from it. Probably the house keys, inferred Cáel.

"My family is in Fort Lauderdale?" she asked, liking the taste of the words on her tongue.

Myra turned to her when she heard the question.

"Cáel, you don't remember? It's so weird that you don't remember us. Fort Lauderdale, Florida? There's mom, me, and Curt. There's our older brother, Carl, and our older sister, Sarah. She's married, got two kids, and you love them, those two!"

Cáel listened. It felt as if she was listening to details of a soap opera family. She furtively tried to study her young sister's expression. Myra looked hurt that she had no recollection of all of them. She wondered if she had a dad. Was he dead? Two brothers. Two sisters. Images floated through her mind, so real that she was taken into the experience as though she was reliving it. Images- solemn faces, a middle-aged woman was sobbing softly. A group of teenage children consoled her, but they were crying themselves. She was one of them, those children. Her knees felt weak. A shard of anguish, perhaps a residue from years ago, jolted Cáel and she felt the force of emotions making her slump back in her chair. She let out a moan, tears flowing unbridled from her eyes to her chin.

"Cáel, Cáel sweetheart, there, there..." Amanda held out a napkin for her. "I wish I could offer you some alcohol, it would made you feel so much better." Amanda poured herself another glass. "Drink up the juice, you'll feel better."

"Listen, Mindy, we need to talk."

"Hey, you called me Mindy! You remember that. You're the only one who calls me that; you, and Dylan, of course."

A flash of an athletic African-American man assailed Cáel. He was slapping Amanda hard across her face.

Cáel cringed and asked, "Whose Dylan?"
"Dylan's my boyfriend," Amanda replied, her expression turning skeptical.

Angry voices traveled through Cáel's head. In her mind's eye she saw Amanda howling hysterically, "You cheating bastard! I fucking hate you! You think I'll forgive you again, don't you?!" She was throwing herself on a handsome black man dressed in a casual sports jacket. Her arms flailed wildly as the man shoved her back on a red couch and stormed out of the door.

It happened here, in her apartment. *She's in an abusive relationship, the fool,* Cáel concluded inwardly, deciding not to ask anything. Amanda was going through her third glass of wine as though her life depended on it.

"You should hit the sack, you know," Myra said. She hadn't spoken much in a while. "I think I'll crash too."

Pushing her chair back, Myra got up and gave Cáel a kiss on the cheek. "I hope you're better tomorrow. We can discuss our plans, I think you should come back to Fort Lauderdale with me... and call Mom!"

Myra disappeared down the hallway.

"Why don't you sleep too?" Amanda said to Cáel, between gulps of wine. "You've had enough for a day, and sleep will do you good. Chris will be here to see you tomorrow. He hasn't been able to visit you at the hospital, you know, with the court hearing and stuff, he was tied-up."

Cáel gazed at Amanda. Chris. It was an important name, she knew that. Was he the father of her baby? She heard a voice in her head, "Stop! You will not get away with this!" It was the same voice — hers. She shut her eyes, and took a deep breath.

"Amanda, is Chris the father of my baby?"

"Oh no, Chris — Christopher Bush, he's your good friend! He... was... Michael's friend. You know, Chris and Russell have been cleared of all charges."

I wish she'd stop saying 'you know, you know'! I know nothing! Cáel's thoughts were shrieking. She wanted to stop Amanda. The names were getting jumbled up in her brain... Chris, Michael, Christopher, Dylan, Russell. Cáel wanted to ask Amanda about the Chinese guy — the Chinese guy who was zipped up and left behind.

"Mindy..."

"What?" Amanda was slurring now.

"Can we just talk?" Cáel's head was throbbing like a giant pulsating bag of worms. "Oh, I'm so tired... there was a guy, in a body-bag..."

Amanda glanced at Cáel, then quickly looked away. She said softly, "You don't remember what happened at all?"

"What exactly happened?"

Amanda looked trapped, like the idea of talking was all of a sudden frightening to her.

"I'm tired, Cáel. It's been a hell of a... You're tired too, let's do this tomorrow. We'll talk later, I promise," she said and got up, tottering a bit, picked the plates, and dropped them in the kitchen sink. Then she started to rinse them, her back to Cáel.

A wave of fatigue engulfed Cáel, and she felt grateful at the suggestion. She left the kitchen to go to the toilet. When she came back, Amanda was settled on the red sofa in the living room, the glass of wine was in her hand, the bottle was on the floor next to her, within reach. Cáel hung around in the doorway watching her. Amanda was staring at the television that wasn't on.

"Amanda?" she said, after a few minutes.

Amanda looked up, startled, like she'd forgotten Cáel was even there.

"What?"

"Where do I sleep?"

She scrunched up her eyes, trying to gauge what Cáel meant.

"Use the room on the left," Amanda slurred in a tone that said, 'leave me alone.'

Cáel realized then that her best friend drank too much too quickly and could be a potential alcoholic. She turned mechanically and left Amanda alone with her bottle. Padding down the corridor, she walked past Amanda's bedroom to another door on the left. It was ajar. She peeped in and found that it was the spare bathroom. It felt strange — like trespassing — walking around in someone else's home. The last door that marked the end of the slender hallway beckoned her. The guestroom.

She pushed open the light laminated wooden door. A dark space greeted her, inviting her into its unfamiliarity. She blinked; she could make out the outline of a bed. Myra was lightly snoring on one side.

She made her way to the bed, unsure, and sat down facing a large bay window. The only light coming into the room was from there. Cáel saw a manic glow far out, the bright glow of the Las Vegas city lights. It lashed out into the darkness of the night, refusing to be scorned. She abruptly remembered that Las Vegas city could be seen from outer space. Strange, she thought, how easily she recalled inconsequential facts, but couldn't remember details of her own life.

The world's biggest neon sign was that of the 'Cowboy in Las Vegas.' She could see it now. Looking at it, she was suddenly sucked into another flashback. She remembered the first time she had driven into Las Vegas, in the night. She had been able to see that sign from miles and miles away, it was a fixture in the night sky for hours, and she had wondered if they were ever going to reach Las Vegas.

They. Cáel sat-up straighter. There was someone else with her in the car. He was driving, in fact. She shut eyes tightly, trying hard to remember more, for she knew that person was significant to her.

"Oh, Lord, are we ever going to reach there? That mean cowboy's teasing me, Michael, drive faster!"

In her memory she was giggling. The man next to her was grinning fondly. She had him in her vision, it was clearing slowly... it was the man in the zip-bag! Cáel gasped and opened her eyes with a start.

Michael! His name is Michael. She tried to recall something more, anything that gave her a clue about who he was. Nothing came to her consciousness.

Cáel finally gave up. She was drained. "Tomorrow... Tomorrow," she promised herself, dragging herself under the sheets and instantly dozing off into a dreamless deathly sleep.

CHAPTER 4

"She doesn't remember anything."

"How much have you told her?"

"Nothing, Chris, I've left the explaining for you to do."

It was nine o'clock in the morning. Cáel opened the bathroom door a bit. The voices reached her, cutting through the morning haze which bathed the little apartment. It was Amanda's voice and another — a man's voice, familiar to her from the elusive miasma of her memories. For a second, she thought she was having another flashback, for these flashbacks were coming faster now and they were more and more real, like she was not living in the actual world, but a surreal, alternate reality. She pressed hard on the doorknob, testing its existence. Satisfied, she moved through the corridor toward the sounds.

"Is she up?"

"I think so. I heard the water running in the bathroom."

"Damn it, the son-of-a-bitch is gone, and left us to clean his mess!"

"Shhh... Chris. Shut it, she'll hear you!"

Cáel tiptoed to the living room, startling Amanda and the male visitor standing in the foyer. She gawked at the man. She realized that it was the guy from the ambulance.

"Hey, you're up, I was uh, just about to come and wake you..." Amanda mumbled. Her face was puffy and she had dark circles around her eyes. Cáel scrutinized her face. Probably hung-over, she thought.

Her scrutiny was shifted now to the man in the room. He was short and muscular, with close-cropped blond hair. He had intense blue eyes, wait no; his one eye was greenish, giving him an eerie appearance. His nose looked like it had seen a few bar-brawls in his younger days. He was dressed in jeans, sneakers, and a brown round necked T-shirt which clung to his well-built frame, showing off bulging biceps. A pair of metal dog tags hung from his neck, the kind soldiers wore, informing Cáel silently that he was enlisted. A red baseball cap graced his head and threw a sharp shadow over his face.

"Cáel, how are you, doll?" The man was moving toward her. In a second, she was enveloped in a warm hug. A few seconds later, he pulled back and looked deep into her eyes, concern marking his handsome, rugged face.

"I'm f… fine, okay, I guess," Cáel let out a sigh. "I'm sorry, I don't remember things well."

"It's all right, sweetheart, it'll take some time."

Amanda, who had been standing like a struck

bird, abruptly darted forward and chimed in, "It's Chris, Christopher!"

Cáel sat down heavily on the bean bag, shaking her head. A memory of Christopher jarred her like an electric charge. She was standing next to him in a kitchen. He was cooking spaghetti in a reddish sauce. There was a sense of sadness in the memory, and she felt the anxiety of that evening scene in her body. A shiver ran through her. She looked around for Myra.

"Where's Myra?"

"She's gone down to the chemist's. She wanted to pick up your prenatal vitamins for you," Amanda answered. "Let me put on a pot of coffee." Amanda excused herself, passing a look to Chris, whose eyes were trained on Cáel's face. He nodded at Amanda, and then sat down close to Cáel.

"I don't know where to begin..." Christopher's deep husky voice was soft, like a lullaby.

"Who were you two talking about, Chris?"

"Who? When, I'm sorry, I..."

"Just now! Tell me!" Cáel demanded angrily.

Chris was quiet. He was nodding slowly, fidgeting with a thick platinum chain around his right wrist. He was avoiding the answer.

"Michael," Chris said finally, his voice staccato. His expression was grim.
Michael. Mike... the man from the zip-bag, the man who she drove with that night into Las Vegas. Swiftly, things were clearing in Cáel's vision. She had a clear flash of Michael and herself. They were kissing passionately. She could feel his tongue deep in her mouth coaxing her into surrender. Mike held her face in his warm hands, his lips insistent on hers, both soft and hard at the same time.

Perspiration broke out of her temples as she relived the flashback.

"Why hasn't he come to see me, Chris?" Cáel vaguely understood that she knew the answer to that question deep down inside. But she needed to hear it, needed to confirm what she already knew. She could feel a growing sense of foreboding inside her. She tried to keep herself calm, for she knew that hysteria, an arm's length away since she'd returned from the hospital, always triggered dumbfounding confusion within her head.

Chris studied Cáel's face for a long moment. Then he whispered, "Because he's dead, Cáel. He's gone."

The Earth stopped moving just then. At least that's how it seemed to Cáel. "What? How? When?" Tears flowed relentlessly from her eyes. Her baby was fatherless before he was even born! She thought of that peaceful, cute guy in the body bag. Michael was dead.

Amanda was back with three steaming cups. Two were coffee, and one was milk, for Cáel, balanced on a tray. Three long cinnamon sticks stuck out from each cup. She was unable to meet Cáel's gaze.

***

Cáel sat mutely a long while, sipping the hot liquid in the cup in her hand. It tasted mildly of cinnamon and settled heavily in her stomach, but it did the job. She felt rounder around the edges, no longer bristled. Amanda and Christopher were closed and distant, each gone to some far away thought in their minds, one with the silence in the room.

"How did he die?" Cáel's question shook both Amanda and Christopher out of their trance. Christopher fixed his intent gaze on Cáel, his eyes boring into hers.

"We were together at my place, hanging out, he had come to see you from Texas. My roommate, Russell, he was having a bad argument with someone on the phone. Then he ran out with a gun. We went after him — Mike and I — to stop him. There was a scuffle. The gun fired, and the bullet went through Michael's chest."

Amanda, who had been hushed, explained, "You heard the gunshot and ran out see what was happening. You tripped on the carpet, your head hit the furniture, and you passed out. That's how you ended up in a coma."

Amanda stopped, searching Cáel's face. It was incomprehensible; she was simply staring at the rug. Amanda continued, "Lucky for you, Chris was there and called for help in time. He saved you." Saying this, Amanda unfolded her legs from the couch and announced, "I have to get to the radio-station, Cáel. Chris and Myra will stay with you."

Bloody escapist, Cáel indicted Amanda, her eyes following Amanda all the way into her room. In a minute Amanda was out with her yellow tote, ankle-length boots encasing her feet. She came up to her and hurriedly kissed her cheek. "You be good, babe, I'll see you in the evening!" She then added, "Oh, the detective from the case called. Detective Davis. He's going to come by to take your statement. Your nurse from UMC is coming too, for a check-up."

In a breeze Amanda was gone. A heavy silence impregnated the room. Cáel got up and started pacing, trying to decode what she had just heard. It was a little too much to take. Her head was starting to throb again. Finding no solace, she sat down again, feeling defeated. Christopher got up and put his arm around Cáel's shaking shoulders.

"Baby, take it easy. It's all over now."

"It's not over!" Cáel suddenly screamed. "It's all just starting! And it has no end, because I don't remember anything! Do you know how that feels to not know the beginning or the end? To just wake up one day and realize you have no past and no future!"

She was breathing rapidly. All the pent up frustration was pouring out of every pore of her being, threatening to smother her and dissolve her into oblivion. She felt she was like a caged tigress, and the key was just out of reach.

She left the room, walking unsteadily down the hallway. She entered her room, shut the door, and slumped down to the floor, her back against the door. The floor felt awfully cold under her jeans. Her palms flat on the tile, her head hanging low, she started to cry. Uninhibited tears flowed down to the tile beneath her.

CHAPTER 5

Her mind stretched back to four months prior, when she had been slumped in dejection just like this, this time on the bathroom floor of her own home, a pregnancy test in her hand. A transparent pink positive in the indicator window had left no doubt in her about her situation.

It was very late in the night; Michael was asleep in her bed, just beyond the closed door. And she was weeping.

I don't want to have a baby.

Cáel had wished she wanted to, but she couldn't fool herself, that's not how she had been brought up. She had struggled most of her life — for money, for space, for an education, for friends, in fact, she could not remember ever not struggling. Living with a mother who was a strong and powerful personality, Cáel had grown into a tough and ambitious young woman, a fighter and a survivor.

At twenty-seven years of age, finally, she liked where she was in her life. She'd got her own home in Las Vegas, a beautiful little condo, and she'd just bought a gleaming new car. Her job was great; she worked with a big airline as a public relations manager. She had just enrolled herself into the University to study Psychology. A wonderful life was kissing her feet. The last thing she wanted was a baby to slow her down. But at the same time, she could not help feeling ashamed of the negative reaction she was displaying to the news. She tried telling herself that it was natural to feel that way. She was too young to have a baby.

Squatting there on the bathroom floor, Cáel was utterly consumed with dread and ashamed of it. Had I not been an extremely active participant in the creation of this new life? It was a product of the seed of love that I have sown with Michael. I love him, he loves, and everything would be fine, she had told herself.

She had finally lifted herself up and dried her tears.

***

The reminiscence came and went. Cáel sat slumped and she cried for a long time, cried over her memories — still so disintegrated over Michael's death, over all that was now lost forever.

Then finally, she stopped, and a prayer escaped her lips silently. It surprised her, she didn't remember what faith she belonged to, or what her ideology was with regard to God. She felt unsure as to how to proceed. She decided she wanted to pray to The God who was omnipresent, who had saved her baby, and who would show her direction. She said a prayer for Michael, for her baby, and for herself.

There was a sharp knock on the door. It was Myra. She heard her soothing voice.

"Cáel, are you okay? The detective is here."

Cáel opened the door, wiping her face with her hands.

Soon she was back in the living room with Myra. Christopher sat across from the detective and her nurse. She had met Detective Davis once before, when he had visited her in UMC to question her after she had regained consciousness. She had not been very helpful back then and had not recalled anything.

He nodded at Cáel, took her hand firmly, gave it a quick shake, and then sat down across from her. He was a tall, sturdy, and a completely bald white guy from Las Vegas PD, dressed in a casual shirt and trousers, but he had the air of a typical law enforcement officer. Her Philippine nurse, Jocelyn, from UMC had been kind enough to visit her at

Amanda's home, and she was checking her vitals while the detective waited.

"You're doing all right, Cáel," said Nurse Jocelyn, prying open her eyelids and studying her eyes with a tiny flashlight. "Your blood pressure is a bit on the higher side though. You have to take it easy with things for a while."

Cáel nodded. Jocelyn turned off her flashlight and pressed Cáel's temple, where a bruise was turning light, from deep purple. The nurse turned to Christopher.

"Mr. Bush, please inform her employer that she is taking a month's leave of absence." Turning back to Cáel, she said gently, "You need to start your counseling sessions with the psychologist ASAP, once a week. Continue with your medication and come in for a checkup at the hospital in a week."

Cáel mutely nodded again. Nurse Jocelyn smiled and let herself out. Myra came over to her and settling down next to her sister, pressed her hand softly.

"Miss Darcie, I'm sorry for bothering you again, but do you recall anything of the night of the accident?" Cáel registered that the good detective was speaking to her, and she looked up from studying her fingers.

"I... not much, Detective. I can't recall anything clearly...," she replied to him.

"Nothing at all?"

"Uh, I... I think the gun fired accidentally," Cáel answered and then looked at Christopher, unsure. Christopher was sitting silent, his face bland.

The detective bobbed his head up and down brusquely.

"That's the conclusion we've come to as well. Russell White, the accused has been acquitted.

He had a great lawyer who argued his case well." Detective Davis paused, and added, "I know you've been through a lot. I've learned that the deceased, Michael Chan, was your boyfriend?"

"Yes."

"I'm sorry for your loss." Detective Davis got up and gathered his papers.

"Miss Darcie, if there's anything else you remember, here's my number. Call me." He handed Cáel a business card and made it to the door. Then he turned around and said, "Michael Chan's body was released from police custody a day ago. His family arranged for transport back to Lubbock, Texas. His funeral is the day after tomorrow in Lubbock. I thought you might want to know that."

Saying this, the detective was gone.

Cáel, Myra, and Chris sat there, voiceless, for

a while. Then Cáel spoke up.

"I want to go to his funeral."

"What? Uh, Cáel, I don't think it's a good idea." Christopher looked unsettled, and his eyes turned to Myra, looking for support. He fingered the chain around his wrist again.

"He's right, Cáel," Myra said, looking concerned.

"Why?"

"Well, for one, you're not well enough to travel. Secondly, I fear his folks won't take your presence kindly."

"I don't give a shit!" Cáel was furious. Her basic nature was that of an honest, but stubborn, person who was taught to fight for her rights by a family that had been through troubled times, and that nature had just kicked in, automatically. "I have every right to be there.

I'm carrying his baby."

Chris sighed in exasperation.

"Cáel, do you really want to put yourself through the turmoil?" Myra reasoned softly. "If you're going anywhere it should be to Fort Lauderdale, with me."

"I'll come to Fort Lauderdale, after Lubbock," Cáel asserted in a tone that meant she had made up her mind.

"Fine, Cáel, you're way too stubborn to argue with. But I will come with you. Let me book two tickets to Lubbock," Christopher said as he got up.

"One ticket, Chris, I'm going alone," Cáel declared with finality.

CHAPTER 6

Lubbock, situated in the northwest Texas, was incorporated in 1909, and since then has become the center of commerce, medicine, education, and culture for west Texas and eastern New Mexico. It's rightly labeled the 'Hub City' of the multi-county region known as the 'South Plains.' The area is the largest contiguous cotton-growing region in the world. Lubbock is also home to three universities and a legendary ranching and music heritage. It's a city of industry, technology, oil, and agriculture.

Cáel exited from her flight at the Lubbock Preston Smith International Airport as the sun plunged below the western horizon. She pulled her jacket close around herself, against the chilly breeze which greeted her with a gust, loosening strands of curls from her hairband.

Here I am, she thought, clutching her shoulder bag, making her way through the other travelers, toward the baggage section in the arrival lounge. The airport looked familiar, for she had been there a couple of times with Michael, and Cáel acknowledged with slight amazement, she knew her way around quiet well. "It's amazing I know exactly what to do at an airport, but can't remember the slightest helpful detail about my own personal life!" she concluded to herself.

As she walked out of the colossal glass doors of the airport, she had a remembrance of a similar day. She saw Michael waiting outside for her, a big bouquet of red roses carelessly tucked in his arm.

She stopped walking and stood still for a few seconds, living that moment from the past. Michael had kissed her, taking her in his arms, and she had felt weak with longing and need. Then, moving away from her, Michael had held the door of his car open as she settled in.

Sweet Mike, why aren't you here? Cáel

questioned inwardly as she waved a cab.

She rattled the address for Hawthorne Suites to the driver. It was the hotel that Christopher had booked for her. She sat back as the cab raced down Martin Luther King Boulevard toward Marsha Sharp Freeway, studying the city that whizzed by, hoping to recall some forgotten pieces of her life with Michael. Cáel saw a big Wal-Mart outlet and instantaneously recollected shopping trips along with Michael to that place. They always argued about who would pay the bills. She shook her head, Good moments... Oh God, why him? Is it my fault? Tears threatened to pour forth as she asked herself that, but she obstinately blinked them away.

Twenty minutes later, she was checking into the hotel.

***

After learning about Michael's funeral, Cáel had had no time to make a trip to her own house, and had hurriedly packed whatever she could find suitable in Amanda's messy wardrobe into a suitcase, while Christopher booked a flight to Lubbock. Christopher had insisted on accompanying her, and Myra had tried her best to dissuade her sister from traveling alone, but Cáel wanted to be on her own to gather her thoughts before she met with Michael's family. Finally Myra had given up and booked her flight back to Fort Lauderdale, but only after she had made Cáel promise that she'd soon follow her.

Christopher had driven her to McCarran International Airport. En route she had asked Christopher questions about Michael and her.

"Chris, how long were Mike and I together?" It felt ironic that she had to ask someone about the details of her love life and the father to her child, and she had grimaced at the turn of fate that had got her in this situation.

Chris shot her a quick glance and turned his

attention back to the road.

"A year," he'd replied.

"I have met his family, right?"

"Yeah, you've visited Lubbock a few times. Mike was based there after his tour to Afghanistan got over, and he had enrolled into Texas Tech University for a course in structural engineering," Christopher replied, somewhat short.

He was in the army, thought Cáel. *Of course he was!* A memory of Michael came floating back. He was coming out of the airport, in his uniform, his dog tags swinging as he rushed toward her, picked her off the ground, and swung her around once... twice... Tears stung her eyes as she remembered Michael's smiling face, merging with his face in the zip-bag. *He's dead! Gone forever!*

Cáel turned to Christopher again.

"Did he live with his folks?"

"No, he had bought a house in the same locale, a five minute walk from his folk's home."

"And? What can you tell me about his family?"

"Well, you've met them. His dad's an artist, he's very good. His mom runs a small shop in the town. She retails in Chinese goods — curios, oriental herbs and spice, all that kind of stuff. He's their only kid. They emigrated from China when Mike was a child."

Cáel wracked her head, trying to recollect their faces, or bits of conversation with Michael's parents, anything that could give her a clue about where she stood with them. Nothing came to her memory.

"Um, Cáel," Christopher said after a long pause. "They don't like you."

"Excuse me?" She was mystified.

"I mean, they didn't exactly approve of Mike dating a brown chick. I don't want to bias your mind before you meet them, but I feel you should know this. They're traditional in their take on dating, and they actually wanted Mike to get involved with someone who was Asian."

Cáel stared at Chris, open-mouthed, suddenly losing the fascination in meeting the Chan's.

Chris continued, "Why do you think I didn't want you to go there? You've still got time, Cáel. You don't have to do this."

She was perturbed by this revelation, but every fiber of her being wanted to be there at Michael's funeral, to say her last goodbye to him.

"I'm not going there for them, Chris. I'm going there for Mike, and for myself. I have to pay my last respects to the man who loved me, and probably died because of my mistakes."

"He didn't die because of your mistakes. Where is this coming from? Stop blaming yourself, you don't even remember your life with the guy, for Christ's sake!"

The rest of the drive went by in silence. Soon they were at the departure. Chris helped Cáel with her luggage and gave her a hug.

"Give me a call when you reach the hotel," Christopher dug deep into his pocket and pulled out a cell phone, "Here, keep this, you can reach me or Amanda, in case anything goes wrong."

Cáel had nodded, and taken the phone.

"Please call me, whatever time of the day or night, if you need me. You sure you're going to be okay alone?"
She had nodded again, and returned Christopher's hug.

***

At the Hawthorne Suites, Cáel settled in her room, a decent-sized space with a comfy, huge bed in the center, facing a large screen plasma television. She put it on and flicked through the channels blindly, her mind on the upcoming morning. She pulled out the Chan's address from her bag. It read:

1988, 74th street, Lubbock, TX

Cáel stared at the little piece of paper, lost in deep deliberation. She felt she was at point zero in her life. As if having no memory of twenty-seven years of her life wasn't enough, the love of her life was dead. She was carrying a dead man's child, who was an Asian. Asian. And she was black. What sort of a life will a half-Chinese, half African-American fatherless kid have? Will he or she face the cruelty of racism and the humiliation of color discrimination? Would she be able to fill in the shoes of a single mom? Cáel questioned her abilities and recognized that she was scared of the future. The emotion gave birth to a feeling of disappointment in herself.

It was an old feeling; it had slunk up on her unexpectedly many a times in her life. Despite having no reminiscence of the times when she had felt the feeling, Cáel could taste its familiar acrimony and gauge its alliance to her psyche.

As much as she hated to admit it, she was terrified of the next couple of days. She was unsure of meeting Michael's folks. Did they know about the pregnancy? They had to! Were they aware of her current memory loss? She doubted very much. *Perhaps they blame me for Mike's death, after all, he was in Las Vegas to meet me, when the bullet sucked the life out of him,* she thought to herself. Should she go and meet them tomorrow? She was in two minds about that. Cáel knew she was free to take the easier way out — to simply show up at Mike's funeral and leave straight for the airport from there — no uncomfortable conversation with the Chan's. But she also knew that the easier way was not always the right way. She let out a sigh.

Tomorrow, Cáel decided.

She got off the bed and opened her suitcase. She pulled out a long black chiffon dress, with a closed neck and long sleeves, and hung it on a hanger. Then she pulled out black stockings and a gray stole, laying them on a dresser next to the wall. Satisfied, Cáel went into the bathroom and ran a shower for herself.

CHAPTER 7

A bunch of pristine white-lilies in her arms, Cáel stood rooted to the ground for what seemed like a long time, though it had just been a few seconds. The taxi had dropped her at 1988 74th Street. What she saw in front of her was a decent-sized double-story house, one of the many on the street; a pea in a pod of similar looking peas, those regular three-bedroom, two-bathroom, spacious kitchen units. Quality housing at a reasonable price. The small area skirting the house was trimmed and well-maintained.

There were a few people standing outside the door to the Chan residence, who were now staring at her with distasteful expressions. Probably friends of the family, thought Cáel, deciphering the looks. She presumed some were aware of who she is and didn't welcome her presence.

Expressions had stopped fazing her a long time ago, and Cáel took a few deep breaths, walking up to the group.

"Hi, are Mr. and Mrs. Chan home?" she asked a somber-faced middle-aged lady standing by the entrance to the house. The woman nodded.

"Yes, you can go inside."

Cáel pushed the door open gently and stepped into the foyer. The house was silent, shaded in drapes. The foyer opened into a small parlor with walls washed in a soft shade of peach. Flowers in baskets and vases filled the room. Cáel looked around for a casket, for Michael. All she saw were a few people sitting around.

A young man looked up as she came in.

"Cáel!" He got up and approached her.

Cáel was foxed. She did not remember him. By the time she could react, he was hugging her.

"How are you? I heard about your injury," he said. "I didn't think you'd be able to make it."

"I... I... Sorry. Do I know you? I have a bit of a memory crisis after the accident." Cáel couldn't recollect him and felt it was necessary to explain.

The man smiled a sad smile and nodded imperceptibly.

"I'm James, James McAdams. I'm Mike's close friend. We've met before, during your previous visits. Uh, I guess your memory's playing tricks," he tried to joke. "Anyway, I'm glad you made it... It's been such a sad event."

"James, how are his parents doing?"

"They are not too good, especially his mom. I'll let them know you're here."

Cáel looked away as James went up the stairs. She could hear the other guests in the room whispering. She felt ill-at-ease, and there was a knot in her stomach. She tried to not listen and focused her attention on the pictures on the walls. They were beautiful paintings of exotic birds and flora, rendered in the most vibrant colors of Mother Nature. Instinctively, she knew they had been painted by Michael's dad. An oriental carpet on the floor complimented the paintings by hosting similar colored birds-of-paradise motifs. A teak-wood dining table graced the dining area, next to what seemed like a roomy kitchen. A polished wooden cabinet with a glass façade was filled with crockery, a visual extension of the dining-table.

"Hello, Cáel."

Cáel swung around to find a graying man with distinct Chinese features coming down the stairs. There was an air of deep melancholy about him, which stirred her and she instantly knew she was face to face with Michael's father. A wave of anxiety engulfed her as soon as that realization took hold. She expected a storm of harsh accusations and braced herself for the onslaught.

Shen Chan, Michael Chan's father, reached the bottom step and stood facing Cáel for a few quiet seconds, looking into her eyes with his sad ones. Then he came forward and gave her a warm hug.

Cáel was both confused and immensely touched. She hugged the old man back and cried along with him. There were like that for a couple of minutes, giving each other a piece of their sadness and solace.

"I'm so sorry, Mr. Chan," she managed to say, leaving her fears behind and feeling relieved at the warm and genuine gesture Michael's father had made to her.
Shen Chan stepped back and studied Cáel, taking the lilies from her.

"How are you doing? We got to know you had

sustained injuries in the accident and suffered a memory loss," Shen Chan was walking to the kitchen, Cáel behind him.

"I'm doing better, Mr. Chan. I still can't remember much. The doctor says that my memories will come back in time, though."

"You shouldn't have traveled alone, Cáel," concern evident in his voice. "Would you like something to drink?"

"No thanks, Mr. Chan, I... I had to come to Mike's funeral."

Mr. Chan nodded in understanding; his expression was resigned as he opened the faucet and filled a glass vase with water. He placed the lilies in the vase and then poured chamomile tea in two cups. Cáel studied him, discerning quickly that she had a good relationship with her boyfriend's dad, not because she could remember much, but more because of his warmth and easy acceptance of her being in that house. She felt herself wanting to hug him again for not holding her responsible for Michael's death.

A memory flashed in her head as she gazed at Shen. She was in the same house, same kitchen. Michael was in the living room, taking pictures of Shen's artwork. Shen was sautéing thinly sliced vegetables in a wok, simultaneously working on a dark sauce on the other stove. Cáel was next to him helping with boiled black eggs — she would always help Shen in the kitchen. They were laughing and sharing jokes as they cooked.

"Ha ha, I must say you're a quick learner, Cáel!"

"Thank you, Shen. At this rate I shall soon be cooking Chinese food really well!"

A prim, small Chinese lady — Michael's mother, had walked in just then, and said that she hoped it wouldn't come to that.

She had been unsmiling, and her rancor had left Cáel stunned. Michael was equally taken aback in the living room.

Along with the flashback came the feelings of great unease. *Chris was right, they didn't want me around Mike, especially Mrs. Chan,* Cáel remembered with desolation.

"How is Mrs. Chan holding up?"

"Not too good, I'm afraid," replied Shen. "She's been a wreck since the news. We've just received Michael's... body. It's been hard on her. It'll take time. I'm just taking this for her, why don't you come along upstairs, you can meet her there. She's not feeling strong enough to greet guests."

Cáel followed Michael's dad, unsure, the anxiety creeping back gradually. They entered a bedroom which was dark, all curtains drawn. Li Juan Chan lay on the bed, propped up on two pillows.

She looked pale and withdrawn, her small body shriveled, and her oriental face, once so pretty, was a mask of gloom. Cáel dimly acknowledged the striking resemblance Michael had had to his mother. She could see the same features on Li Juan. As she recognized Cáel, those features hardened for a fraction of time, then relaxed in despair. Cáel went up to her and took her hand in hers, gently. Li Juan Chan didn't pull away.

"Mrs. Chan, I'm so sorry," she said to her, softly.

Li Juan said nothing. She stared at the opposite wall for a while, her eyes distant. Then all of a sudden, she turned to Cáel.

"Were you with him... in his last moments?" Tears ran down the old woman's cheeks. Cáel moved her head in affirmation.

"I was," said Cáel, simply, "but I can't remember anything. I hit my head."

Li Juan's tone turned caustic as she said, "So convenient, isn't it, girl? Call my son there and then forget it ever happened. Except, my son dies, dies! Nothing is going to bring him back!"

Shen Chan shook his head in misery, and addressed Li Juan gently. "Juan, it's not her fault."

"Mrs. Chan, I'm very sorry, I... I wish it had turned out different. The concussion has blocked out all memories of my life and of my life with Mike," Cáel's voice was breaking and she said, "I don't recall anything about the most significant person in my world!" She burst into tears.

"You are a damned soul," Li Juan Chan whispered. Then she added bitterly, "You'll be fine, Cáel, don't worry, you're young, time will do it's sponging on you. Soon you'll be prancing around with a new lover."

Cáel was now sure the elderly couple had no idea about her pregnancy. She vaguely wondered why Michael hadn't given them the news. She decided that they needed to know about it as early as possible. After all, the baby had their blood flowing through him, or her.

Li Juan's discourtesy had unnerved Cáel. It was too much to absorb after Shen Chan's warm embrace. She made up her mind to break the news after the funeral. Shaking under Li Juan's attack, Cáel excused herself from the bedroom and, saying goodbye to the apologetic Shen Chan, she promised to be back in the evening for the vigil service.

***

Michael's body was at the funeral home, in accordance to the Chinese custom which states that the elders of the family don't carry out the last rites of a younger man; it's a task for the offspring of the dead. Therefore, if an unmarried man dies, his earthly remains must be left at the funeral home. His parents are not allowed to take the body home or even to offer prayers for their son. These are jobs reserved for the children of the deceased.

Shen and Li Juan Chan belonged to the Catholic faith, and Michael's last rites were performed in conformity to their religion. The vigil took place at the funeral home and it comprised of a Scripture Service of readings, reflections, and prayers for Michael. Some of Michael's close relatives, who also lived in US, arrived in time for the service. They shared stories and eulogies about Michael. Li Juan and Shen held hands in mutual comfort as people remembered humorous instances and fond tales. Li Juan was softly crying, her grief overwhelming all attendees in the hall, and most of all, Cáel.

Cáel mutely prayed for strength for Li Juan to help her tide through her immeasurable sorrow. She prayed for fortitude for herself as well, to face the very real fact of Michael's demise.

Next to the priest lay the casket, open. A string of rosary had been placed in Michael's hands. Cáel walked over to the casket during the vigil, and placed a rich red rose in full bloom, on Michael's chest, a solitary tear escaping her eyelids as she said a prayer for him. She gazed for the last time at his peaceful face. That face had been her world, a world she didn't know anymore.

"Goodbye, Michael. I'm sorry..." Cáel said softly to him.
Prayers and Hymns, led by the priest, were sung by all, followed by a touching remembrance by James, honoring the life and gifts of Michael. The service ended with closing words by the priest.

CHAPTER 8

The day of Michael's burial was rainy. Sullen clouds had told the sun to stay away, drizzling teardrops of rain as the bell tolled through Michael's funeral.

There was a funeral mass held at St John Neumann Church. It was a private ceremony, attended by men and officers of Michael's unit at Lubbock and close friends of the Chan family. The gathering was a blend of Army uniforms and mournful black. Several of the young men in uniform nodded or greeted Cáel, none of whom she could place in her fragmented mind, but presumed that she'd met them at some point in her past with Michael.

As she moved past the last pews, a familiar face caught her eye. It was Chris, looking almost unrecognizable in uniform, one among the many young brave men present there to acknowledge the occassion.

He decided to come. I'm glad, she thought, as their eyes met in understanding. He lightly touched his cap with his gloved hand, as she sadly smiled at him.

Cáel sat in the front row with Shen and Li Juan Chan, as the priest opened the ceremony with a prayer, "As Christians, we celebrate the Christian funeral to offer worship, praise, and thanksgiving to God for the gift of life which has now returned to God. The celebration of the funeral rites is a way to remind us of God's mercy and to bring hope and consolation in a time of crisis..."

The prayers began as everyone in the pews opened their copies and read together, in connivance with the Catholic custom at the funeral Mass, where readers sit with their families, and are invited forward by the priest when they are to proclaim the readings — one person for the Old Testament reading, one for the New Testament reading, and third for the prayer of the faithful.

After the psalm response and Gospel, the priest asked Shen and Li Juan to offer the bread and wine, symbolic of the body and blood of The Lord.

Members of Michael's mother-unit who were not on duty in Afghanistan were present at the funeral Mass, stiffly standing apart in their uniforms, in the last pews. There was a six-man honor guard along with them, to give Michael an apt military funeral. Tradition, honor, and dignity are the hallmarks of a military funeral, and the guard followed all ceremonial aspects that are usually performed at the grave site, whether the service member died while on active duty or was honorably discharged or retired, whether he or she attained the rank of admiral or was newly enlisted.

A member of the honor guard was discreetly standing, in full-uniform, at the funeral service. When the casket was closed, the guard covered it with the flag of the United States of America. The priest led the procession out of the church, pallbearers carrying Michael in his casket. It was important for the funeral cortege to start on foot. It was then carried forward by a hearse.

The flag-draped casket arrived at the Restheaven Cemetery and was carried to the grave by the uniformed men of Michael's unit. Three volleys were fired by the firing-party as a gun salute to an American soldier. After that the honor guard lifted and held the American flag taut over the casket as the bugler sounded "Taps." The six men ceremonially folded the American flag into a triangle and handed it to the highest ranking officer present there.

The officer presented the folded flag to the Chan's with a brief statement of gratitude and a salute. They carried out every detail of the ceremony with cadence and precision. The priest then read the committal service at Michael's graveside. Michael was buried under a Mimosa tree, its lavender flowers carpeting the ground around the grave.

Cáel picked up a handful of mud and threw it over Michael's coffin, tears welling up in her eyes and blocking her sight, as Christopher came up beside her, placing his arm over her shoulder, and applying gentle pressure.

They slowly walked back to Christopher's rented car.

"You didn't tell me you were planning on attending Mike's funeral, Chris?" Cáel asked him.

"I wasn't. I came only to support you. I wanted to see if you were alright, Cáel. You didn't call at all yesterday," Chris pointed out.

"I'm sorry. I know you're concerned for me, Chris. It's just that, I was caught up with the vigil. Chris, I don't think Mike's parents know about the baby. I find that surprising. Why didn't Mike tell them?"

"I don't know, maybe because his mom would

have creamed him for being so careless! He was mamma's boy." Then he turned to her and asked, "What are you planning to do now? You can come back with me tonight."

"Chris, I want to tell the Chan's about the baby. I'll spend today with them," she said, decisively.

"You know, Cáel, you actually don't have to do that. It can be a clean break from the past," Chris forcefully suggested to her.

"I don't want a clean break from the past. The past is all I have right now, Chris. It's okay if you don't get it, I don't expect you to. I have to do what is best for my baby."

With that one statement, Cáel put a stop to anymore discussion on the subject.

"I get it," Chris said abruptly, ending the conversation. He turned his collar up against the wind and got inside his car.

"See you in Las Vegas," and he was gone.

Cáel drove back with Li Juan and Shen in the Limousine. They were all quiet during the drive, each coping with their loss alone. The family was gathered at the Chan's house for a luncheon. It was a solemn affair and wound up quickly. Throughout the afternoon, Li Juan Chan did not exchanged a single word with her, looking through her as though she'd been manufactured in a glass factory. Once the guests had left, she got herself busy with the cleaning, a rock of silence and bitterness.

Cáel stayed on to help the Chan's with the winding up and the dishes. She took a deep breath and decided to break the wall of ice with Li Juan Chan.

"Mrs. Chan, it will get better. I know nothing I say will ease your pain, but I want you to know that you're not alone in this."

Li Juan was silent, mechanically wiping the

plates and putting then aside. Then unexpectedly, she started to speak.

"It doesn't make sense, us living here anymore. We should go back. At first this place was great. Now the bills keep skyrocketing, the shop keeps getting broken into, nothing will get fixed. We can't get any help with our problems. There's no one to look after us. Mike's not here anymore, we should go back... we should go back. Shen! Shen, why don't we go back to China? We can start again..."
Cáel watched her in alarm as she trotted out of the kitchen, speaking incoherently, and looking for her husband. She went after Li Juan and found her in the parlor, Shen's arms around her, holding her tight. Li Juan was crying again.

Cáel took a deep breath and stood back, not wanting to interrupt the intimate moment between the old couple. After a few minutes, she decided it was time to tell the Chan's about the baby.

CHAPTER 9

"Mr. and Mrs. Chan, there's something you need to know… I, uh, I'm pregnant, I'm carrying Mike's baby. I'm four months into term."

There was no easy way to say it, so Cáel decided to hit the nail right in the head.

There was pin-drop silence in the room. Shen and Li Juan both gazed at Cáel with unreadable expressions. Then they looked at each other for the longest time. Cáel squirmed in her shoes, wishing if only she could fast forward the excruciating minute.

Then an uncertain smile lit up Li Juan Chan's face. It was followed by a smile on Shen Chan's face. Cáel looked from Li Juan to Shen, back to Li Juan, a slow smile lighting up her face as well. A hundred birds chirped inside Cáel's soul — birds of paradise, as she grasped the full significance of the news to the Chan's. She was suddenly lighter, almost flying over the clouds, and she admitted to herself that the Chan's acceptance of her pregnancy meant the world to her.

"Cáel, I'm speechless," said Mr. Chan. "Li Juan, did you hear that? That's unbelievable news!" Shen Chan was somewhat animated. "Four months? Why didn't Michael tell us?"

Li Juan shook her head slowly in bafflement, trying to find the right words to say. Words came out with some difficulty. "Probably because we had disapproved of his relationship with Cáel in the first place," she said sorrowfully. "It all seems so silly now... he's gone forever. I'd take it all back, if I could!"

A fresh burst of anguished tears prevented Li Juan from speaking further. Shen put her arm around her and shared her pain, silently.

"Come and stay with us, Cáel, while you're in Lubbock, let's talk more about this," said Shen, after a few minutes, weak with emotion.

Cáel nodded, agreeing immediately, and thus they sat for a long time, finding strength and comfort in each other, trying to comprehend the unpredictability of human life.

***

Cáel went back to the hotel after spending an hour with Michael's parents. She felt tremendous sadness for them and was thankful she had been able to ease some of the agony with news of the baby.

She smiled as she thought of the baby. It was precious to some other people in the world, too! Not just her! She sat down on the edge of the bed and gently ran her hand over her tummy.

"I love you," she whispered to the tiny life growing inside her.

Before checking out, she decided to call Christopher and tell him the news.

"Hey Chris, its Cáel!"

"Hi doll, how are you? You okay?"

"I'm fine. I've just got back from Mike's folks' house. Chris, they are thrilled about the baby! They've asked me to stay with them!" Her relief was infectious. Unfortunately, Chris wasn't reflecting it at all.

"Cáel, I don't think it's such a good idea. They never liked you, and they are too conservative to accept an illegitimate child!"

Cáel was stung.

"Chris, don't ever call my child that," she warned Chris angrily. "Even if they never liked me earlier, they've put their reservations away at this moment of great grief, and if you cannot fathom that, then I have no more to say to you!"

Cáel hung up and stormed about in the room seething. His words were so insensitive, so hurtful. Michael had just been laid to rest and Chris had called his child illegitimate. It was cold, callous. Then, realizing that strong reactions weren't good in her pregnant condition, she calmed herself down, refusing to let his stinging words get the best of her. She packed her suitcase, having already decided to check out and spend the night with Michael's parents. She was hungry and went down to the hotel restaurant. She ordered a light dinner; it was late evening and she thought about the night ahead.

Soon she was back at the Chan residence and was shown into her room by drained and pale Li Juan.

"I hope you'll be comfy, Cáel. I'm sorry, it's not very plush."

"Mrs. Chan, please don't worry about anything, it's perfect."

Cáel gave Li Juan an involuntary embrace and said goodnight.

***

Li Juan made her way down the stairs and found her husband sitting in the dark living room. She silently sat down next to him, and slipped her shoes off.
"God is giving us Mike again," Shen Chan said after a while.
"Through a person I've only resented since I met her. Every time I think about 'what could have been' I feel shattered," Li Juan replied sadly, the grief of a thousand lost opportunities riding her voice.

"That is the beauty of hindsight, Juan," Shen replied pragmatically, "It all might've turned out different had we let go of our prejudices. It's all water under the bridge now."

Li Juan was silently weeping. "We were trying to push Mike toward marrying somebody else. Imagine, if that had happened — what would have become of Mike's baby? He wouldn't have been a part of our lives."

"Let it go, Li Juan. Cáel is going to be an important part of the rest of our lives. It's time to start afresh. Let's do the best we can, and let the Lord show us the way from here."

Shen helped his wife up, and together they made their way to their bed, ending the most wretched day of their lives.

***

"Was Mike religious?"

It was next morning, Cáel and Shen Chan sat under the small porch after an early morning breakfast. She had questions about the man she had loved, and who better than his father to tell her more about Michael.

"He wasn't religious as religion goes," Shen replied after a minute. "He believed God was not in dogmatic scriptures or in statues or prayer beads. He believed in a Universal Entity, The Supreme Being, or The Light.

"Our family ancestors back in China followed Confucianism. In China, Confucianism is more a way of life than a religion. It's a cultural philosophy which pervades into the very core of Chinese principles. When I was a child, my parents turned to the Catholic Church, as many people did at the time, at least in urban China. Soon our religious life became an amalgamation of our original ancestral thought-process combined with Catholic rituals. We moved to the US when Mike was eleven. For a long time he wrote, 'Atheist,' under the heading of religion, in all the forms he'd fill. He refused to believe that Christ is the only path to God.

"It was when he was in Afghanistan that he started praying — he said that things were going to get a lot worse before they got better, and he needed to pray to something or someone greater than mankind — The Omnipresent. War changed him."

Cáel chewed on that for a while. She felt what she had heard was the essence that summed up what made Michael the man he was — tough, yet so gentle.

"Did he always want to be a soldier?"

"He was awfully good at everything he ever did, that boy. A straight 'A' student at school, he was very mechanically inclined. Then one fine day, he came home from college, and told us he was enlisting, and that he wanted to serve the country for a few years. His mother wasn't too happy about it, but Michael wouldn't budge. Six months later, he was on a plane to Afghanistan.

"Our life was harsh in China, personally and socially. I was a struggling artist and Li Juan found it difficult to make ends meet in the paltry amount of money I made. For a long time, our marriage was turbulent, and we didn't have children. Michael was born after four miscarriages. He was the most precious thing in the world for us."

"How did you come to US?" Cáel asked Shen.

"I struck a business deal with a traveling businessman from Texas; he had liked my paintings. For a couple of years I was selling him my artwork, which he retailed in an art gallery in Texas. That's when I got exposed to the idea of America and the seed was sown. Then Li Juan inherited a little house from her parents. We sold it, and suddenly we had a small fortune. We used that cash to immigrate and set ourselves up in the US. Li Juan opened a small shop here, and I retailed my paintings from there for a while. We came to America to give Michael more opportunities in life."

"Was the move easy on Michael?" she queried,

picturing a small Chinese boy looking lost in school.

"It was daunting. Michael had difficult teen years, adjusting to a new society where he obviously stuck out like a sore thumb. He had to work hard at his relationships in school, but soon he was doing splendidly well. Something like you, Cáel. You two had plenty in common," finished Shen, swigging the last of his tea.

Cáel was quiet. She barely knew herself, the events of her recent life had ensured that. Memories of being different unhurriedly flowed into her head like treacle pouring out of the mouth of an inverted jar, coating a burnt toast, overflowing from it into a plate. She closed her eyes, feeling the slow journey of the memories from the subconscious to her consciousness.

She remembered feeling inadequate. She remembered mean white-skinned girls laughing at her pigtails. She remembered her teacher, Mrs. Ellen Sanders, a full-blown Caucasian woman of Land-owners' heritage resenting her for her grades. She remembered getting ragged for being smart.

Cáel had a vision of her twelve-year-old self, sitting with an old man, reading a children's book under mellow lamplight, a rustic rug covering their knees. My Grandfather, she recollected. After reading the story, her grandfather had elucidated to her the moral of the fable. He had then explained to her the importance of working hard in school and taking her education seriously.

I had to struggle too, just like Mike, Cáel mulled silently. I have to ensure our child doesn't.

CHAPTER 10

A Ford SUV came to a halt in front of the house, discontinuing the flow of Cáel's thoughts. It was James McAdams, Michael's childhood buddy.

"Good Morning Mr. Chan, Cáel," he greeted, bounding up the pathway toward them. "How are you and Mrs. Chan? I thought I'd just check in on my way to work."

James sat down on the porch step as Shen Chan said, "I'll tell Li Juan you're here."

As Shen went in, James turned to Cáel, shaking his head.

"I can't believe Mike's gone, he was larger than life at twenty-six years."

"You and he have been friends a long time, right?" she asked.

"Almost fifteen years. I can't look back into my life without thinking of him. He's everywhere. We were brothers to each other. He always had my back. The most helpful and honest soul I've ever met," James remembered. "You're staying awhile?"

"Maybe a few days," Cáel shrugged. She wondered if he knew about the baby. "James, did Mike tell you about the baby?"

"The baby? Uh, no... What baby? Are you pregnant?" James appeared surprised.

Cáel nodded. "He kept it a secret. I wonder why?" After a pause, she said almost to herself, "Maybe we had decided to keep it a secret..."

"Maybe," echoed James. "Mike was sort of occupied with work and studies last few months. We weren't catching up that frequently. He had made a couple of trips back to Vegas, to see you, I suppose. He was the kind of guy who needed his space, you would know. I never asked too many questions, unless he wanted to talk."

"Where did he spend most of his free time when he was here?"

"Mostly at his house, it's close by," said James, pointing his thumb in the direction where Michael's house was, presumably. James went inside to chat with the Chan's, leaving Cáel staring in the direction where he'd pointed.

She thought for a bit and then went in to speak to Shen.

"Mr. Chan, is it okay if I spend some time at Mike's place?"

"Would you like me to go with you?"

"Thank you, but no. I'd like to have some time alone there."

"Very well," Mr. Chan said quietly.

"I understand. I'll go get the key for you. Michael gave us the spare, just in case he ever locked himself out."

***

Mike's house was a stone's throw away from his parents', at least for someone with a good throwing arm. From the outside, it looked just like the Chan residence. A wind chime hung under the porch. It was gently swaying in the breeze, the soft notes of melancholy welcoming Cáel as she stepped into the shade.

She opened the door and entered slowly. The first emotion that she experienced when the fragrance of the air inside sailed into her nostrils was a familiar longing and love. It surged through her at breakneck speed. The emotion was peppered with excitement and desire. Memories, a million of them, catapulted and jumbled through her brain pockets. She relived all the occasions when she'd entered the same house in Mike's arms, and she could almost sense him next to her, a warm reassuring presence.

Mike's house was similar to his parents, but done up in a sparse and modern fashion. Warm colors were splashed on the walls. Cáel ambled up to the dining table, and noticed little knickknacks and personal items — keys, post-it strips, a Swiss-knife, a half full mug of milk, carelessly left here and there by Mike. Probably just before he left for Vegas, to see me, she thought, wretchedly.

There were photographs all over the walls. Pictures of her and Mike, radiantly beautiful pictures of two beings in love with each other. Michael was an alive and vibrant image, his handsome face smiling, and his posture youthful. His strong, capable arms encircled Cáel's waist in most of the photos.

The kitchen was neat and, on the refrigerator door, Cáel saw notes and to-do lists written in a small neat hand, amidst photos of her and

Michael's parents.

Cáel walked to the bedroom on the first floor. She opened the door and took in the atmosphere. It appeared as though the room was paused in activity. She could sense his energy everywhere. Michael's uniform was hung in a hanger over the closet handle. Shoes lay here and there, a towel lay on the dresser. His perfumes and combs had been used and left in a hurry.

A huge color blow-up of her face hung on the wall above the bed. Diamonds sparkled like stars in her ears. It was a recent photograph, and Cáel immediately remembered the day when Mike had clicked that shot. It had been her last visit to Lubbock, when Michael had picked her up at the airport.

It had been her birthday — the first of September, and Michael had surprised her with diamond studs. They reached home, and cracked open a bottle of expensive wine.

Michael loved taking her pictures and, sure enough, even that evening he had clicked several. One of them was on the bedroom wall.

They had spent her birthday in each other's arms, inseparable, unable to stop their love for each other. That was the night she got pregnant.

The big king size bed was unmade, covers thrown backward. Cáel had a compelling vision of herself and Michael just then. They were naked, covers and bodies entwined, on that bed, making intense love, their hands caressing each other in dark shadows. She felt his kisses on her skin, and it sent goose pimples on her back and thighs. So real was the flashback that she had to sit down, weak in her heart, and yearning for Michael's touch.

Michael's sweatshirt lay casually flung on the bed. It said 'Texas Tech.' She picked it up and brought it to her cheeks, rubbing the soft fabric on her face. It smelt of a scent that was infinitely known to her, Michael's smell, a mix of cologne and his natural skin's fragrance. Tears crept into Cáel's eyes and she slid to the floor, the sweatshirt close to her chest. She was heartbroken, but content for now, to be in the same space where Michael had lived.

Cáel felt she was home. Despite suffering the loss of Mike more than ever, she was delighted about all the compartments and spaces of memories that were opening in her mind.

She went over to Michael's study table and opened his laptop. The desktop wallpaper staring back at her from the screen was a picture of her and Michael next to a serene lake. She remembered that picnic. Michael had taken her to the lake, to make up for the previous evening at his parents' house. It had been her first visit to Lubbock, right after Michael had taken a house and settled in. It was also the first time she had met Michael's parents.

The occasion had left her stunned, because Michael's mother, Li Juan, had been downright rude the entire evening. When Cáel had entered their home, she had stood leaning by the kitchen door, glaring at her like she was contemplating whether she should shoot Cáel, or poison her first and then shoot her. Cáel had smiled at her, but she had stared back in a blatantly suspicious manner. Li Juan had barely exchanged ten words with her the whole evening, and when she and Michael got back to his house, Cáel had been furious.

"What was that all about?"

"What?"

"Your mother, that's what!"

"Oh, don't mind her, she'll come around."

"Come around to what?"

"Come around to accepting the fact that I can date a black chick, if I want to date one."

"You could've warned me, at the very least! I was worried there — she was about to beat me with her broomstick!"
Michael had been mighty amused at Cáel's reaction. He had grabbed her and made her sit on his lap and kissed her till she was no longer furious at him.

Cáel smiled at the memory of that night.

She went through all the pictures in Michael's laptop. There were pictures of them in Fort Lauderdale, where they had first met one another, and of Cáel which she had sent to Michael over the course of the six months that he had been in Afghanistan. Then there were snaps of them in Las Vegas and in Lubbock, once Michael had returned. The pictures were still scenes of their life together — of her shopping for veggies when Michael was in Las

Vegas with her, of Michael doing yard work, and her helping him with his new house in Lubbock, of them doing homework together...

Cáel missed Michael bitterly, as memories of fun and contentment came back to her. She sat with the laptop for a long while, reliving the frozen moments. Then finally, she sighed and closed the computer. She went into the bathroom and filled the bathtub with hot water to which she sprinkled bits of all the bathing salts and oils Michael had on his shelves. Remembering that pregnant women are advised to not have baths in bathtubs, she shed her clothes and stood in the fragrant water. She ran the shower and stayed in there a long time. She soaped herself with Michael's bar of soap, remembering the scent on him. She shut her eyes so she could feel it all the more, realizing it's true what they say — the best things in life are experienced with your eyes shut.

When she came out, she was light, heady and

permeable, as if the air was moving through her, like she was like a clean, blemish-free white kerchief fluttering in the wind.

She slipped into Michael's sweatshirt, wanting to wear nothing else but that. It was warm and bulky, enveloping her into a cocoon of security. She got into Michael's bed, smelling his pillows deeply, a spicy scent of his aftershave filling her olfactory nerves. Cáel pulled the covers over herself and fell asleep, dreaming of Michael and their baby.

CHAPTER 11

Was it possible to fall in love with the same man all over again? Twice? Even though he was dead? Because in the two days that Cáel spent at Michael's house, she fell deliriously and maddeningly in love with him all over again. She wore his clothes, slept in his bed, wore his shoes, and felt a luminous energy ascend from within her core, all the way up to her brain, igniting all her senses. Cáel felt healed and at peace within those loving walls of the enchanted place, never wanting to step out again. She understood it was too early to get over Michael's demise, but she also knew that she had started to walk that road.

Therefore, when it was time to leave, Cáel wanted to take along with her all that she could of Michael. Pulling out a suitcase from Michael's luggage, she filled it with some of his clothes and perfumes, and also packed his laptop and some photos. Then she set course to the Chan's house, wanting to spend the morning there, then catch her early afternoon flight.

Li Juan was dressed in a casual skirt and top, and she appeared smaller and stooping to Cáel, grief had robbed her of her formally upright bearing. She had prepared a simple breakfast of Chinese eggs with salty pancakes with some Chinese accompaniments, and both of them were waiting for her. Li Juan appeared drained, the tragedy of losing her son telling on her face. Looking at their faces, Cáel could instantly sense that they wanted to have a serious conversation with her. Shen greeted her warmly, Li Juan hesitant but not cold, and the three sat around the dining table to eat. Cáel helped herself to the dim sum, steamed dumplings of delicately wrapped baby shrimp. No one spoke immediately, as conversations on the breakfast table in the Chan's home were supposed to follow a regular pattern and not take anyone by surprise.

"Cáel, why are you in a hurry to leave,

darling?" Shen asked her after his plate was empty, between mouthfuls of dim sum.

Cáel did not reply immediately, unaccustomed to explaining her movements, especially after the memory loss. At length, she replied to him.

"Mr. Chan, I have to get back and sort out the mess in my life. I have to check in at work, or at least file for leave. And there are other things... I have to get my memory back," Cáel replied candidly.

"Actually that's what we want to speak to you about," said Li Juan, pouring herbal tea for everyone and sitting down to have her breakfast.

"You're pregnant, maybe you should take it easy, you know. Why don't you stay here with us? You can stay in Michael's house."

Cáel was mildly taken aback by the idea, because Li Juan of all people suggested it, but mostly because it was so interesting, and she hadn't thought of it. "Can I do that? Is it possible?" she asked herself.

"You could continue staying at Lubbock in Mike's home and bring up the baby here, close to us," Shen was speaking to her, stressing on the idea Li Juan had just introduced. "We'll take care of you like our daughter, Cáel, and Mike's son would be our own."

Cáel was tempted. She was tempted like a hungry weary traveler is at a shady orchard of exotic fruit. But she also understood that she had a whole forgotten lifetime to sort through. Miles to go before I sleep, she told herself.

She smiled at the one word in Shen's statement that had caught her attention. Son.

"How can you be so sure it's a boy, Mr. Shen?" she queried.

"It will be! I'm sure of it; it's going to be Mike coming back to us. Your baby is God's gift, Cáel!" Li Juan insisted in a voice tinged with mild desperation.

Cáel understood how important her pregnancy had suddenly become for the grieving couple. She knew that in China and other oriental cultures that followed the patriarchal family system, every couple wished for a boy; for they believed that it was a male issue that carried the dynasty forward. The desire for a boy was so ingrained in the people, that sometimes women underwent multiple abortions, until they were pregnant with a male fetus. Cáel wondered if they would love her child the same if it were a girl. She would still be a part of Michael.

Combined with that latent thought process was the fact that Shen and Li Juan had just lost their only son. In their thrill at the news of the baby, they were trying to shrug the grief of their loss off their tired shoulders. They were pinning all their hopes and dreams on this unborn child. Cáel felt a wave of empathy for the old husband and wife. She wanted to ease their minds, but at the same time, she wasn't herself very sure of the future, and didn't want to make hollow promises.

"Mrs. Chan, whether it's a boy, or a girl, I promise that the baby will be a big part of your life, regardless of where I live, I'll never keep him, or her, away from you," Cáel reassured them.

"But we'd like to be there for you. Have you planned on where you're going to deliver? Who will take care of you immediately after your delivery?" Li Juan questioned, "Becoming a mother and then fulfilling that role is a tough ride, it's no piece of cake," she added gently.

"I understand that now more than ever, believe me. I haven't really thought about it after these recent events, but most probably I shall continue to consult my original gynecologist in Las Vegas. I don't want to change too many aspects of my life for the obvious reasons, you see. Don't worry, I'll be in regular touch with you two, and I definitely would like you to be there for the baby's birth."

"I think you've made up your mind, Cáel, but you must remember, we are here for you," Shen said as he got up from the table, signaling the end of the debate. "Let's get going, or you'll be late for check-in."

***

Shen and Li Juan dropped Cáel to the airport. It was a fifteen minute drive, during which Shen chatted away with Cáel, but Li Juan was quiet.

"Cáel, please remember, the offer to stay here is always open," reminded Shen, helping her with the luggage.

Li Juan was suddenly teary-eyed. She had just

lost her son, and now with Cáel leaving with Michael's unborn child was hard to bear for her.

"Cáel, my child, it is impossible for us to bring back the lost time, but you must find it in your heart to forgive me, for Mike's sake," her voice wavered as she spoke.

Cáel understood that Li Juan was referring to her previous hostile bearing which Cáel could only compare to the vibe one got from righteous old black churchgoing mamas who would whip your behind if you ever dare trespass their kitchen gardens. Cáel had long reconciled and forgiven Li Juan for it.

"Mrs. Chan, please don't say that. What's happened in the past is done and over with. You'll always be the grandma to Mike's baby. Let's start a brand new relationship with this new life, and take it from there," Cáel reassured the old lady and gave them a hug.

"It's Shen and Li Juan, not Mr. and Mrs. Chan," Shen said as he returned Cáel's warm embrace. Cáel smiled and nodded. Saying her goodbye's to the Chan's, she set off for the airport with a heavy heart.

***

Amanda was at McCarran Airport to pick Cáel up. It was nice to see her standing outside, dressed in a splash of color, as usual. Cáel grinned at her as she came closer. Despite the huge task that lay ahead of Cáel — of getting her life back on track without Mike — she felt good to be home in a city she loved.

"You look better! I can almost see my perky old friend in there somewhere," Amanda remarked as she backed her car out, heading southeast onto the Airport Connector Road.

"I feel better. Mike's funeral was the first step to closure, I think," Cáel spoke thoughtfully. She added, "I hope you're taking me to my place, Mindy, I want to get started on things, enough of moping and staggering!"

"Cáel Darcie has definitely arrived!" Amanda was happy to hear the old twang in Cáel's tone. "Your place it is!"
They were now belting down Bruce Woodbury Beltway. Amanda turned right onto the Las Vegas Expressway, and soon they were in Black Mountain, Henderson, zooming past the golf course and the country club.

Cáel's condo was in a three-story building of six apartments, two on each floor, one among the many on that street. All units had a garage on the manicured grounds around the construction. Cáel felt happiness gush through her as they entered the tiny driveway to her garage. A little brass plaque said 'Cáel Darcie' on the awning over the garage door.

My home! She was looking forward to a few days of recuperation in her own space with memories of Mike, before she started work again.

Amanda handed her keys to her sixth-floor apartment in the elevator. The keychain had a glimmering metallic mermaid hanging from it.

Cáel unlocked her home and stepped in. It was as if she had also unlocked the door to millions of memories which they came floating by rapidly, a train of colorful compartments, whizzing through the tunnels of her unsettled mind; happy, vivid, magical memories which matched the colors of her home.

Warm ochre and amber washed walls greeted her as she entered. Wooden masks of aborigines and handicrafts of Red-Indians grinned back from those walls as though thrilled to have their mistress back. Carpets, rugs, and cushions in shades of maroon graced the teakwood floorboards. Bright sunlight lit the rooms, hindered here and there with light muslin drapes in various shades. The entire décor of her condo was a celebration of color and character, and Cáel was delighted to be a part of it. She walked from room to room, touching a shelf here and caressing a chair there.

"I'd like to drink something, let's see what's in your fridge," Amanda broke her trance, and Cáel suddenly realized she wasn't alone. She had totally forgotten Amanda for a few minutes.

They trooped into the open kitchen, and Cáel pulled out two bottles of fruit juice, offering one to Amanda. Amanda downed it in one go and then picked up her embroidered satchel bag.

"I've got to get to work; I'm up on the radio in an hour. Why don't we have dinner together?"

"Sure, let's eat here, I'll make something nice!"

"Will do. Catch you later," Amanda said as she

slid out the door.

Cáel leaned over the granite worktop of her kitchen in peace, studying her home and reveling in the recollections it brought back, mostly of her and Michael. She had a flashback of her working in the kitchen, cleaning up and after dinner. Michael had come up behind her, holding her, nuzzling into the nape of her neck, moving her hair aside, kissing it and murmuring in her ear.

"You need help, baby?"

"No, and you're distracting me!"

"Let me help you and then take you to bed, my love."

"You go on, this is a woman job, and then you can do the thing that men do!"

She had pushed him away playfully.

Cáel soaked in the tingling sensation that memory had triggered and padded into the bedroom to see photos of Michael she remembered nailing up on the wall.

She walked into the room to find that the wall was bare. Naked nails were hammered into it, with no photos hanging. Frowning, Cáel went to the bathroom, hoping to see Michael's toiletries and scrubs.

Nothing. With growing alarm, she yanked open the closet in the bedroom. It had been Michael's, she could recall clearly. It was empty. There was no sign of his clothes or shoes.

Cáel was baffled. Michael had spent a lot of time with her in this apartment, why was there no sign of him? She pulled out her laptop from her bag to find that there were no pictures of him, or them, anywhere in her hard drive.

She started to hunt for Michael's belonging all

over her home. It took hours of her time, but it was a futile search. Nothing came up. It was almost as if he had never been a part of her life in Vegas. And it was a huge contrast from Michael's home in Lubbock. His home had been like a sanctuary of their love.

Something wasn't adding up. Why was Michael erased from her life?

CHAPTER 12

Amanda came back to Cáel's place straight from work, to find her slouching on the sofa in total darkness, sullen and brooding.

"What happened now?" she asked, zapped at the complete change in Cáel's demeanor from the exuberant mood she had left her in.

"Mindy, there's something all of you are hiding from me?" Cáel asked in a low, dark voice.

"May I put on something that'll illuminate this place? I can barely see you in here!" Amanda leaned over a lampshade and switched it on. Soft yellow light filled the room. Amanda parked herself next to Cáel. "What do you mean?"

"There's no sign of Mike in my house. No photos, no notes, no cards, nothing at all that says I was involved with someone called Michael Chan. Why? I don't understand."

Cáel's face had the look of a bunny rabbit in the middle of a highway, frozen in the glare of a speeding car's headlights.

Amanda let out a deep sigh.

"Mindy, there's something wrong, isn't it? Please, tell me! I'm making a fool of myself!" Cáel searched Amanda's face with her doe eyes. Amanda took her time replying.

"Cáel, babe, there's no easy way to tell you this, and it's so ironic that you don't remember — you and Michael broke up in the beginning of November last year. Right after you found out you were pregnant," Amanda said softly, her voice full of compassion.

Cáel gazed at Amanda unblinking, her face a large question mark. Amanda continued after a pause.

"After your accident, you couldn't remember anything, and gosh! Now there was so much to tell you! I thought I should wait awhile before I told you this, you know, I wanted you to get some of your mental strength back. I was kind of hoping your memory would come back on its own."

"But why? Why would we break up, right after learning about my pregnancy? Did he know? Had I told him about the baby?" Cáel's questions were an anguished cry.

"Cáel, my dear," Amanda was feeling acute sympathy for her friend and words were coming slowly. "The baby was the reason you two broke up. You see, he didn't want this baby. He wanted you to get an abortion."

Cáel felt as though someone had pulled the very ground from under her feet and she was falling into a dark bottomless abyss.

Abortion?
Tears flowed copiously from her eyes, and her throat was a salty well of hurt.

"I… don't… no, it doesn't make sense, Mindy. He was Catholic, how could…?" Cáel was finding it tricky to formulate all her thoughts and doubts into the appropriate syllables that sounded like words.

"It was a nasty surprise for you, Cáel. We all thought the world of Mike, but he had fallen from grace. He didn't want to commit to the relationship."

"But… we were in love, Mindy! I know it was real. I can feel it in every bone of my body!" Anger was now slowly replacing the feelings of betrayal and abandonment.

"It sure appeared that way, babe, but he bailed out on you. You made a choice, Cáel. You decided to keep the baby. Actually Chris was a tremendous support to you during this crisis."

Hot rage slowly filled Cáel, pressing sharply against the membranes of her head and heart, and she picked up a crystal bowl lying on the side table and flung it at the far wall. The bowl crashed into a thousand pieces which were strewn all over the floor.

"He betrayed me! What kind of a man bails out on his own child?" Cáel was seething, her voice a screech. She couldn't believe her ears.

"Cáel, honey, calm down. You were done with him, you were getting on with life. Don't beat yourself up about it now. This is not good for the baby!"

Amanda walked over to the water dispenser and got Cáel a glass of water. Then she grabbed an unopened bottle of red wine and helped herself.

Cáel sipped on the water, her head a smoldering volcano.
"Here I am, living and breathing Mike, loving and worshipping him, and I come to know he was just another spineless jerk. What is wrong with me, why can I not do anything right?"

Cáel was now suffering in another bout of self-doubt and futility, a feeling as familiar to her as the back of her hand.

"Darling, please, don't do this to yourself all over again! They are all spineless jerks. Men are dogs. Look at Dylan! He's attracted to me because of my independence and wants me to depend on him. It gives him a sense of power. When I start doing that, he finds me clingy and distances himself. He goes and screws the first skirt he sees. I start hating him with confident surety and finality, which attracts him to me all over again. It's a vicious cycle, and we can't break out of it because we love each other! Men are dogs!"

Amanda uttered the lines as though they were a holy mantra she abided by and it ended all questions of 'why' in her world.

"Hey, why don't we order food from that new Mexican place?" she said, changing the subject unexpectedly.

By now, the bottle in Amanda's hand was almost empty and she was surfing through the numbers in her cell phone and speaking to Cáel at the same time, "Listen, you have an appointment with the psychologist at the hospital tomorrow morning, ten o'clock. Chris said he'll drive you."

Cáel was deathly quiet. She felt she had completely lost her bearings and coordinates, and felt herself sinking into a familiar sea of self-doubt and pity. Regardless of her recent memory loss, Cáel could well identify with this abyss of misery that had been a part of her since... well, since she could remember, peeking deep into her childhood. Since her father decided he didn't need them, she guessed. Life had been a struggle to conform. To conform to the 'miss-goody-little-two-shoes' white girls from her school. To conform to whatever was the fate of poor abandoned black families. To conform to being a fatherless black girl who was not supposed to be bright, or smart, or successful.

Cáel had a history of making decisions very quickly about men. As a teenager, she had often fallen in love fast and recklessly, always ending in hurt. She had been raised by her mother to be independent, self-sustaining, self-deciding. Since she had entered her twenties, Cáel had been free to make all life-changing decisions at her own free-will. She always felt under pressure to make her life work, to prove her decisions sound.

All points of reference that she'd established about her immediate past were in relation to Michael and their love. With that buoy sunk, she was swept away into stormy seas.
"What a pig!" thought Cáel, "I've just come back from his funeral, deciding to dedicate my life to our baby, and to our love! He was just using me! Oh! I'm glad he's dead! Had he not been dead, I would've killed him myself, I swear!"

CHAPTER 13

The next morning, at the University Medical Center, Cáel was ushered into the psychologist's office. The letters on the glazed glass door said, 'Dr. Monica Sutherland, PhD,' the name of a bright, dark-haired lady in her forties, who greeted Cáel with a handshake. Cáel had had two short sessions with her already, when she'd been in the hospital, recovering for her injury. She liked the warm doctor and felt a familiarity with her that put her at ease instantly.

"How are you doing, Cáel?" Dr. Sutherland asked while quickly glancing through her file. "Have you been able to revive any kind of memories?"

Cáel appeared as though she hadn't slept in a century.

"Well, I keep getting these flashbacks now and then. I've found that whenever I have a relevant sort of a conversation or event, the related memories come back," she tried to explain.

"That's a good sign of a speedy recovery. You are young and strong, so I see no reason why your mental capacities wouldn't get restored. But remember, you mustn't overstretch yourself," the doctor elaborated, then asked quietly, "I understand you're pregnant and have suffered a personal loss?"

"That's right, Doctor. I've suffered an even bigger loss because I just learned that my dead boyfriend had no intention of carrying out his responsibility toward me and the baby," Cáel replied in a voice laced with rancor.

"Had the two of you talked about having a child together before your pregnancy?"

Cáel shook her head.

"No, it wasn't a planned pregnancy," she answered and related to the doctor the events of the last few days. The doctor nodded imperceptibly, listening out, her wise eyes boring into Cáel.

"Unfortunately, I can't remember much of that time," Cáel said in the end.

"Because you can't, you're facing the entire turmoil all over again. It's natural for you to feel upset and lost because you cannot recall most of what happened. At this juncture, it would be best to not take on too much emotionally," Dr. Sutherland said. "I think, for a while, it will be a good idea for you to be with people who are close to you, and who love you unconditionally. Why don't you spend a few days with your family? Parents and siblings have a way of healing bruises, you know?" she said, adding, "Let's meet again next week. I'm sure you'll be feeling much better."

***

When Cáel left the psychologist's chambers, Christopher was waiting for her in the lobby waiting area. She suddenly had a strong sense of déjà vu, seeing Christopher lounging on a sofa, flipping through a magazine.

She had a recollection of a similar scene and clips of many doctor's appointments swam in and out of her consciousness. At the end of each one of them, there was Christopher, waiting for her in the lounge, helping her with forms or picking up her pregnancy vitamins.

Cáel was suddenly thankful to God that Christopher had been with her through all her difficult moments — something his friend Michael should've been doing, she thought. Cáel brushed the thought out of her head instantly. She had beaten herself up the entire night about her relationship with Michael, and in the wee hours of the morning had fallen into a disturbed exhausted sleep. When she woke up, her heart felt cold and empty — she had blocked it all out temporarily. She did not want to think of Michael at all.

With a growing sense of gratitude toward Christopher, Cáel walked out of the hospital building with him into the sunshine toward the car park.

As Christopher opened the car door for her, she leaned forward and gave Christopher a warm hug. Then she kissed him on his cheek. Christopher was visibly taken aback at this show of affection and laughed out loudly.

"Whoaaa… what brought that on?" he asked in his lovely, silky voice.

"All angels deserve some love, Chris," she replied tearfully as she slid into the car seat.

Christopher went around and got in, smiling. The smile on his face made his rugged features appear very handsome.

Cáel clipped her seat-belt on, conscious of

her slightly grown tummy, then turned to Christopher.

"No, seriously Chris, you've been wonderful to me all these months. I didn't realize it until last night. Amanda told me what all had gone down with Mike and me, and how you've been there with me through everything. Thanks."

"Hey, it was nothing. You deserve a lot more," Chris answered, smiling, but his tone was very serious. "You deserve someone better than Mike. He was a great guy, but his fear of commitment got the best of him."

Cáel was in no mental state to converse more on the subject without breaking down, so she changed the topic.

"Chris, why don't we go down to Fort Lauderdale? Do you think you can spare a few days from work? I want to meet my family, and we can hangout, you can show me around, I don't remember much of the city, anyway."

"Yeah, sure. Why not? Let me speak to my Commanding Officer, I'm sure I can manage a couple of days, at the least."

"Great, it's settled then!" she excitedly announced. Then she was thoughtful.

"I should speak to my mother," she mumbled doubtfully, not sure of where the relevant phone numbers were.

Christopher glanced at her and, as though reading her mind, said, "You should. They've been worried sick about you… The numbers are in your address book at home, don't worry. Your cell phone is in police evidence as of now, but since they've closed the case, you'll receive it shortly."

Cáel gave Christopher a grateful smile.

"Uh, Cáel, there's something you should know," Christopher continued. "You haven't told your family about the breakup with Mike.

They think you two were still together."

"Really? Why didn't I tell them?" Cáel's face darkened at the revelation.

"Well, they thought the world of Mike, and, you didn't want to admit you'd made a bad choice. That's how you are. You want to have everything perfect. It's hard for you to admit defeat!"

Cáel silently processed the statement by Christopher in her head.

"Well, turns out I made a bad choice, after all," she said, almost to herself. Then, shaking herself out of the dark thought, she suggested, "Chris, why don't we stop at the supermarket near my place and buy some groceries and veggies. We'll cook lunch at home."

***

Cáel reached home with Christopher and

headed straight for her telephone. There were voice messages from Amanda, her older sister, and her boss. Cáel worked as a public relations manager with Delta Airlines. It was a well-paying job and helped her pay her bills and tuition fees, for she had also enrolled into a Psychology course at the University.

Cáel called her boss, surprised at how easily she could remember names and details from her workplace. After letting him know she was doing better, she asked if it was all right to continue her month's leave of absence. He agreed readily. A persevering and ingenious worker, she was her boss's darling.

Then she picked up her address book. She sifted through the pages till she found the phone numbers she was looking for. Soon, she was dialing a phone in Fort Lauderdale, Florida.

"Hello?" said a clear rich voice on the other end, a voice as familiar to Cáel, as her own.

"Mum?"

"Cáel baby, where have you been? Are you okay? I can't get through your cell and no one answers your home telephone!" Love and concern welled through the telephone and flooded Cáel.

"Ma, I'm fine. I… I was at Lubbock," sadness tinged her tone. She thought of her time in Michael's house and suddenly felt dizzy.

"Sweetheart, it's so sad, it's such a horrible tragedy. You need to come home, baby," her mother pleaded to her. "Let us take care of you."

"I'm coming, Ma. I'll be there as soon as possible," tears poured forth as Cáel spoke, making it difficult to speak further. Memories submerged her as she recalled names and faces of her brothers and sisters, wanting to be there, with them, more than anywhere else.

"How is everybody at home?"

"Everyone's worried for you, sweetheart." Her mother was crying too.

Cáel promised her mother she'd see them all soon and hung up after a few minutes of the emotional dialogue. She was left overwhelmed and depleted.

Christopher, who had been in kitchen and listening to the conversation as he chopped greens for a light meal, came over to Cáel in the living room and held her in his arms. She wept on his shoulder, feeling raw and soothed, both at the same time and glad to have him with her.

CHAPTER 14

As the plane circled around the International Airport of Fort Lauderdale, Florida, Cáel peered down from the window at the beautiful seaside city of her childhood and student days, with its canals and waterways weaving through areas full of opulent homes, as well as picturesque marinas loaded with luxury yachts. Memories careened through her mind of her student days, of outings with her sisters and brothers, and shopping trips with her mother.

Cáel and Christopher collected their bags and headed for a taxi service outside of the airport. Giving her mother's house address to the cab driver, Christopher turned to Cáel.

"Doll, we'll drop you to your mom's and I'll head for my hotel. I'll come by in the evening and meet up with your folks, okay? It'll give you some time to relax and catch up with your family."

She agreed, and her thoughts trailed to her family, pleasure at the prospect of being with them warming up her cold heart.

***

Cáel's mother, Marie Darcie, lived in a spacious four-bedroom, single story house in Coral Ridge, Fort Lauderdale. It was a neighborhood of old-timers and young upcoming professionals, Spanish, black and white, family oriented people. Marie had bought the property fifteen years ago, when she had moved to Fort Lauderdale from Chicago, leaving her husband back there. She had taken up a blue collar job at a large tourist resort in the city and had been lucky to have found the property so cheap and affordable.

Over the years, Marie had worked her way up the ladder in her workplace, now boasting the status of Key Hostess at the resort. A beautiful, well-maintained woman in her fifties, Marie was very proud of what she'd achieved, having started from scratch. She was a strong, self-sufficient person and had raised five children on the same principals.

For many years in her marriage, Marie had been the silent dutiful partner, trudging along behind her struggling husband's preoccupied shadow. She tended to their shabby apartment and rollicking kids in the chilling winters of Chicago, scrubbing, cleaning, and cooking while also working a part-time waitress job, as Frederick, her husband, strove to finish his medical studies, offering his love and affection to his wife and children on the extremely rare occasions when he emerged from his walls of solitary confinement. Every penny of their minuscule income went into his books and classes.

Once Frederick had attained his Doctor's degree, they moved to a better neighborhood, and Marie gave up her job, but her marriage was more depleted than ever, as Fredrick's long working hours kept him away at the hospital.

It was almost as if Frederick had forgotten what it meant to have a family at home, or that he had a wife with emotions, not a robotic caretaker.

After what seemed like an age of misery and loneliness, Marie one fine day decided she'd had enough of the chill that both Chicago and her husband had offered to her and moved down south to Florida with the children to live with her aging father. Frederick and Marie were still married, but now it was simply a union on paper, and the children had no relationship with him.

Cáel was twelve when she came to Fort Lauderdale. In her life, her grandfather was the most influencing presence, taking the place in her heart which should've been her biological father's. He taught her and her siblings the value of living an honest and good, clean life.

Cáel's grandfather passed away when she was in her late teens. It was the first experience of death and loss for her, and it had left an indelible mark on her consciousness.

***

Cáel's reunion with her family in Fort Lauderdale was a moving one, charged with love and emotion. When she entered the door of her mother's house, along with her entered a thousand voices, scenes and moments from her past — her childhood with her family. Memories from back then; quarrels, endearments, smells, and aromas, filled up her senses until she was riding on a swollen wave of sentiment.

She crossed the threshold of her childhood home, into a serene drawing room filled with her brothers and sisters.

They rushed forward to greet her, her brother Carl picking her up and swinging her around. Carl was a criminal attorney and a junior associate at one of the leading law firms in

Fort Lauderdale. Her young brother, Curt, was still at school and lived with her mom.

As Carl steadied Cáel down, her sister Myra came up and held her tight, tears running down from her eyes. Sarah, Cáel's older sister, her Spanish husband, Raul, and her two children, Rafael and Ria, came up behind Myra. Sarah planted a resounding kiss on Cáel's cheek, as her nephew and niece tugged at her arms.

"Cáel, you scared us for a bit there!" said Raul, with a tight hug.

"I scared myself too, but I'm doing so much better, Raul," she replied, smiling through her tears. She looked past Raul, at her mother, who was standing back, letting her brood mingle and patiently waiting her turn.

"Ma!"

Cáel rushed to her mother and embraced her for a long minute.

"My baby! How are you, love?" Marie voice was tearful, as she looked Cáel up and down.

"I'll be fine now, Ma," said Cáel, finding great strength in her mother's reassuring embrace.

"Come, I baked scones," Marie said, as the whole family trooped into the dining room and sat around a teakwood table, filled with food and love. There was something simple and reassuring about food and family eating together. Cáel was home, and she already felt unwrinkled.

CHAPTER 15

At exactly seven o'clock in the evening, the doorbell rang and Marie opened the door to find Christopher Bush, dressed in semi-formals, a big bouquet of roses and chrysanthemums in his hands. Marie welcomed him with a warm smile.

"Chris, come in," she said, accepting the flowers. "Cáel has told us so much about you!"

Carl shook Christopher's hand and introduced himself, as Christopher stepped into the drawing room.

"Hi, I'm Carl, Cáel's older brother. She says you've been a bit of a guardian angel to her!"

"Not at all, I've only been a friend to her, that's all," Christopher demurred, a little embarrassed at the attention and praise.

Cáel came in just then, dressed in a white

cotton sheath dress, looking relaxed and dewy.

"Wow, you look fabulous," Christopher drawled in her ear, as he went up and kissed her gently on the cheek.

"You aren't doing too badly yourself, sir," she complimented softly, taking in the dapper jacket and trousers, and Christopher's neatly combed hair.

 Dinner was a gregarious affair, between the leg-pulling and the family jokes. Christopher fit right in with Cáel's brothers and Raul, and they were ganged up together in making funny one-liners at the women of the family. The pleasant evening came to an end at midnight, and Christopher took his leave, saying goodnight and thanking Marie for the wonderful dinner.

Cáel stepped out with Christopher to see him off to the car.
"Thanks for doing this, Chris," she said, taking

his hand as they reached the car.

"Thanks for what?" Christopher asked, turning to her and taking her other hand.

"Well, for coming to Fort Lauderdale, for one."

Chris looked at her beautiful face in the gleaming moonlight, and said, very softly, "Cáel, I'll go to the end of the earth for you."

A couple of cars passed by on the quiet street. Cáel saw themselves in her mind's eye, as they stood there in the moonlight, holding hands and looking into each other's eyes. To a layman we sure must be looking like lovers, about to kiss, she observed, half-amused. Then it very suddenly dawned upon her that Christopher was in love with her. He had always been in love with her!
Wow, I never saw it!

Then Christopher did something that caught her by surprise. He leaned forward and kissed

her parted lips gently. She didn't react, liking the feel of his soft, seductive lips on hers.
The kiss lasted just a couple of seconds, but it confused her enough to pull away. Michael's face flashed in her mind.

"Chris, I... I'm sorry, I can't. It's too soon..."

Christopher opened his eyes and straightened, "Uh... I'm sorry, I shouldn't have."

"I hope you understand."

"I do... I, Hey, forget it happened, okay?"

She gave Christopher a long look, and nodded. He got in his car, and smiling at her, drove away.

She stood there for a while, rooted to the spot where Christopher had just kissed her. What had surprised her was that she had like it. She wanted to be kissed and loved. Michael's betrayal had left her loathing herself, riddling her with self-doubt and confusion. She badly wanted to erase and do away with that episode of her life, and they best way to do that would be to fall in love with somebody else, somebody kind and gentle, like Christopher.

She thought of Christopher's lips and his seductive, deep baritone voice in her ears. One thought led to another, and she thought of what his body was like, a physical need rising inside her.

She cautioned herself. She knew this wasn't the solution — starting a relationship on the rebound, and oh, what a rebound! She remarked to herself, a relationship with his best friend!

And, of course, there was a baby to consider. Cáel shook her head. Not now, I'll think about it some other time, she told herself and then she walked back slowly into the house.

***

Raul had left early with the kids, but Sarah had stayed back to spend the night with Cáel in Marie's house. They bunked up together in their old room, which was still done up in their teen years' posters and trinkets.

Cáel badly wanted to discuss with Sarah her kiss with Christopher, and the subsequent feelings that kiss had brought forth in her. But all of this was difficult to explain, because her sister didn't know yet what had transpired between Michael and her.

"How is the pregnancy coming along, sweetheart? I hope you're eating right and taking good care of yourself. You're up for a big scan in the coming month," Sarah said, changing into her night clothes.

Cáel adored her older sister. Sarah Darcie Almonte was four years older, an intelligent and energetic nurse; she had an aura of efficiency and compassion around her which radiated into her surroundings. While growing up, Sarah had been her mother's rock and mother-like to her younger siblings. She was mighty and commanding, a star that pointed homeward. She had a ready solution for every single problem, and Cáel and her siblings were awed by their oldest sister's giant presence in their life. She couldn't think of any aspect of her childhood and teen years without seeing her sister Sarah's face in those memories. She had been her support and guiding light through and through.

They were like chalk and cheese, her mom would often say. Cáel was as reckless and impulsive as Sarah was careful and meticulous. Cáel went through her youth, a wild-child, rolling in and out of thrills and relationships, reveling and hurting in life, learning lessons the hard way. While Sarah was steady, stoic, focused, thinking through every decision with care to the consequences.

Sarah had met Raul Almonte at the hospital, when Raul was admitted for a knee surgery.

Raul was a real estate developer. They fell in love, and Sarah embraced everything Spanish, so as to be in sync with her Spanish boyfriend. Raul's family fell in love with Sarah instantly, which is how things went with Sarah always; no one who crossed paths with her could help but love her spirit and perseverance. Raul and Sarah got married in a Spanish church and now had two lovely children. Sarah's life was a textbook ideal for Cáel.

"It's a miracle the baby's unharmed. It's the only thing that's keeping me going, Sarah," Cáel replied at length.

Marie came in with two glasses of hot milk for her daughters. Sitting down next to Cáel on the bed, Marie ran her hand through her curly hair and said, "I'm so sorry about Michael, honey. You went for his funeral; it must've been so difficult for you..."

It was the first time Michael's name had been spoken in the day, and Cáel froze, finding it tremendously difficult to speak. Tears of anger and hurt filled her eyes.

Now, late in the night, Cáel's two stalwart pillars, her sister and mother, were with her, and she did not want to hold back anything, so she let loose all her confusion and disappointment with them.

"There's something I haven't told you guys, I think. I don't remember it, but I've learned that Mike had bailed out on me, Ma. He didn't want the baby. In fact, we had broken up a while before the accident."

"What? Why didn't you tell us?" Sarah asked.

"You've been struggling with your pregnancy alone all this while?" Marie was shocked.

"I don't know why I didn't tell you. I guess I didn't want to admit I had failed. Maybe I wanted to protect Mike."

"Well," Marie said, "You sure did that, because all along, till your injury, you had me believing he's been with you through everything."

"I don't know why I did that! I hate Mike! He was a swine!"

"Cáel, honey, don't overreact," Sarah said gently. "Something doesn't make sense about Mike's decision. He seemed like a grounded fellow. This is not him at all, from whatever I've seen of him. He simply adored you!"

"Yes, he did, and he had us all fooled! I spent two days in Lubbock in his house, with his parents, loving him entirely, even in his death. I came back and this is what I learned! He wanted me to get an abortion! I don't know what to think anymore! I hate him! And I hate myself!"

Cáel dropped her face in her hands and collapsed into tears, which turned into a gasping wail. She pressed her palms on her eyes, wanting the tears to just stop, but they kept coming. Marie was softly crying too, incoherent at the sight of her daughter's grief and finding it difficult to talk.

Sarah moved over next to Cáel and held her close.

"It's okay to cry, honey, it's okay to cry."

CHAPTER 16

It was a disturbed night's sleep for Cáel. She had vague dreams of going into labor, her dad helping her with the delivery, combined with Michael pushing her off a cliff and Christopher catching her. She woke up the next morning with a need to be outdoors and away from her imaginary demons.

She stepped out early, wanting to explore the city, starting with 'Bonnet House,' a 1920s residence converted into a museum. She met up with Christopher at the Las Olas Boulevard, and they had a lovely breakfast of crepes in a cute café on the street.

Las Olas Boulevard was the city's most architecturally unique, authentic, and eclectic shopping and dining district that ran from Andrews Avenue in the Central Business District all the way to Fort Lauderdale Beach, interlaced with canals and waterfront homes. The name "Las Olas" means, "The Waves" in Spanish, and historically, Las Olas Boulevard was an important road, as it was once the only way to reach the beach by land. The commercial stretch boasted of bars, nightclubs, bridal stores, shops, boutiques, art galleries, restaurants and hotels — this is referred to as the "Riverfront" area of downtown Fort Lauderdale.

Fort Lauderdale, for decades, supported the image of an ideal holiday; "teen-agers gone wild" destination for students from all over the country. Located in a spectacular natural setting, where the New River meets the Atlantic Ocean, it's a party hotspot for youngsters, and a delightful setting for relaxing vacations and special events like weddings.

Christopher and Cáel strolled down the boulevard, ducking in and out of cool breezeways, until they reached the ice cream place Christopher wanted to take her to.

"Cáel, this is where I saw you for the first time ever, almost two years ago."

They were standing in front of a quaint little Italiano Gelato joint filled with young college students and couples. As Cáel stepped in, she had a strong flashback of a day almost two years ago — the first time she'd met Michael. So strong was the recurrence, that she could almost taste the figs 'n honey flavored ice cream she'd been helping herself to, back then. She could see herself and her friends in front of her eyes. She had taken her girlfriends out for a treat, as she had just bagged a great job with the airline. It was September, right after her twenty-sixth birthday.

While they had been gorging on the frozen delights, a big group of about fifteen young men had walked in. They were all young, sporting crew cuts peculiar to soldiers in US. Their straight bearing and body language was a telltale sign of their army background. Obviously on a holiday, the guys were having a rollicking time. Many of them, having spied the pretty young chicks in Cáel's group, and had come over and introduced themselves.

Cáel had gone over to the counter to pay for the ice creams. As she was searching for her card in her purse, she heard a voice over her shoulder.

"Ma'am, please allow me."

A handsome young man with oriental features had been right behind her, and before she could reply, he had paid the tab with cash. Cáel had objected to it.

"Oh no, you shouldn't have!"

"Please, it's my pleasure. I'm Michael Chan, by the way."

He had introduced himself, holding out his hand.

"Cáel Darcie."

Cáel had taken his hand, and it was a firm and warm handshake. They had walked together to the seating area. She had wanted to know more about that cute guy.

"So, are you all here on a holiday?"

"Yes, we're going to Afghanistan next month. This is just a holiday to cushion the blow of the grueling six months coming our way."

"Aha, you're in the army?"

"Yup, based out of Lubbock, Texas."

Cáel had studied him, drawn to his drawling Texas accent, as he'd slipped into a low bench across from her. He wasn't very tall, about an inch more than her, but appeared to be extremely fit and sinewy. Thick musclebound arms stretched out from strong shoulders, and an equally thick neck supported his fair, delicately handsome face. He was Chinese or Korean by genes, Cáel had figured.

"What about you? Are you studying?" Michael

had asked.

"Um, I've just graduated from the university, degree in product design. I've just cleared the interview for a job in public relations with Delta Airlines. That's what the party's for," Cáel had replied.

"Congrats! I imagine you're a local?"

"Yeah, my family's here, though I stay on my own in an apartment with a roommate, just to be closer to the college."

"Is the roommate a guy?" Michael had questioned.

"Ha, ha, ha, no! It's a girl, and no, I'm not a lesbian."

"If that is the case, I'd like to take you to dinner assuming no jilted boyfriend is going to turn up with a baseball bat to beat me to pulp later, that is."

"There's no boyfriend, and I'd love to have dinner with you."

***

"Cáel, you okay?"

It was Christopher. His voice snapped Cáel out of her reverie and into reality. She looked at him, bewildered. In the entire recollection, she hadn't seen Christopher. I suppose I never noticed him back then, she thought.

"We met here?" she asked Christopher.

"Well, we never got introduced properly. Michael had all your attention, but I was here too. All of us were vacationing together after our training wound up. We were due to go to Afghanistan very soon. Of course, after that day, we barely saw Mike around because he was only with you, for the rest of his leave," Christopher replied in a mildly regretful voice.

Cáel could feel a now-familiar wave of nausea rising up as she thought of Michael, and all those unresolved emotions started to resurface, searing her consciousness with rancor.

"Let's get out of here. I want to go for a gondola ride."

***

If Cáel had thought she could escape from Michael in a gondola, she was mistaken. Memories of Michael besieged her once again during the scenic ride. Their first date had started with a cruise in the beautiful waterways as the sun had gone down the on the horizon. She could see the entire evening before her mind's eyes, how much ever she tried to distract herself.

Michael had picked Cáel up from her apartment that night. She had chosen to wear a very short off-shoulder dull-gold dress, which complimented her dark complexion and showed off her slim, shapely legs. They had decided to go for a boat ride.

Colorful lights from waterfront places were reflected off the water and had given an ethereal feel to the atmosphere. Mike had cracked open a bottle of fine wine and they had sailed together in the bobbing gondola, enjoying the nighttime beauty of the seaside city as well as one another's newly found company.

They had had dinner in the Casablanca Café, a classy place that had been voted as Fort Lauderdale's most romantic restaurant. Once an old home, the building was restored and turned into an oceanfront café serving American dishes with Mediterranean and Caribbean flavors thrown into the mix. Cáel remembered how much she had enjoyed their first date and how charmed she was with Michael's boy-man demeanor and infectious smile. By the time Michael had dropped her home, she was almost in love with him. That was also the first time they had kissed.

Their first kiss.

Cáel closed her eyes and shook herself out of the trance, determined to not indulge herself in it further. When she opened her eyes, she found Christopher lounging opposite her in the boat, staring at her peculiarly.

"You're thinking of Mike, aren't you?"

"This ride reminded me of our first date. Gosh, it was such a long time ago, and it was so beautiful when we'd had started out. Why did it go so wrong?"

"All good things always come to an end, Cáel… only for better things to start."

"Not every good thing ends, Chris. Mike and I, we were supposed to be different."

"Things changed, Cáel. When you two started out, you were young and unattached, ready to get involved. Added to that, Mike was flying out to a battle zone in Afghanistan. He was living it up real good in his last few days in US. Once he wasn't in the country, it became very easy to maintain a low maintenance, long distance relationship, you understand?"

"Especially with a fool like me, who truly believed in him," Cáel concluded, bitterly.

"No, you were no fool, he was a great guy while the going was easy, you see. I knew him, we were friends after all. His attitude changed only after you got pregnant. Now, the relationship was bordering on real commitment, and he wasn't ready for that."

"Not ready — I can understand. A lot of people have a fear of committing. But asking me for an abortion? That blows ass!"

"You have to take a look at his background to

understand that. It's common to undergo abortions in his native place. His mother had a few abortions before he was born. I don't know why, but I know that their marriage has seen rough times, and they have been unfaithful to each other.

"After coming to United States, he was under a lot of pressure to perform. So much so, that he joined the army, just to escape that constant pressure, until he was sure of what to do in life. He did not ever want to disappoint his parents. Dating you was one of the forbidden things. His parents wanted him to marry a Chinese girl and settle down."

"If he was such a mamma's boy, why didn't he just do that? Why did he start off with me in the first place?"

"Cáel, it wasn't planned. He just fell for you. He had no idea where it was going or if it was going to last."
"Well, he should've thought about that before

he got me pregnant."

Chris moved toward her and settled next to her. Then, taking her hand in his, looking into her rich brown eyes with his intense mismatched ones, never once blinking and spellbinding her, he spoke very slowly.

"He's gone now, Cáel. And you... you can be free. You can fall in love again. Take another love. Marry somebody else... Think about it."

Cáel stared back at Christopher, hypnotized by his silky voice. Then suddenly, she frowned, and her eyes opened wide.

"Oh my god!" she exclaimed, and her hands flew to her tummy.

Christopher straightened with a jolt, alarmed. In a second he relaxed a bit as he saw the expression on Cáel's face. It could only be described as 'happily startled.'

"The baby just kicked. The baby kicked!" she informed him excitedly, the tenor of her voice reaching a crescendo by the end of her uttering. She took hold of Christopher's hand and guided it to her mildly protruding stomach.

Christopher breathed out noisily in relief. Then he concentrated on his palm which was placed flat on Cáel's stomach.

"Oh gosh, I felt it! It kicked again?"

"It sure did. This is amazing!" she giggled. Christopher laughed along with her, totally taken by the unique experience.

They finished their gondola ride as the sun was setting into the lap of the western horizon, and headed back to Cáel's home, their mood uplifted by a little unborn baby's involuntary physical activity.

CHAPTER 17

Christopher had dinner with Cáel's mother and Myra at their home. The conversation centered on the baby and its tiny little toes kicking its mom's tummy, making its presence felt in the world.

Christopher excused himself soon after dinner as he was flying out early the next day. He had to get back to unit in Las Vegas. Making Cáel promise she wouldn't overexert herself, Christopher had kissed her hands and left. Exhausted, Cáel too changed and had headed straight to bed. Adjusting herself in a comfortable position, she pressed her stomach gently with her palms and smiled to herself.

"How are you, my little one?" she whispered to her baby, caressing her tummy slowly, feeling the tautness that had crept in as her fifth month had started. "Can't wait for you to come out, cutie pie... now sleep tight, and don't kick your mommy anymore tonight, okay?"

Marie popped her head in to say goodnight to her daughters.

"Hey, how are you doing, honey?" she asked Cáel, as she gazed at her with fondness, "You look tired. You shouldn't exert yourself, sweetheart."

"You're right, Ma. I guess I'm still getting used to the idea of being pregnant."

"Get used to it quickly, now, and start taking care of yourself. Did you take all your prenatal vitamins today?"

Marie admonished Cáel, sitting next to her, "You should just move to Fort Lauderdale, Cáel. Quit work for a while."

"C'mon, Ma, you know that's out of question. I'm going to be a single mom. That's hard enough, a single mom without a job is harder! I can't quit work!" Cáel said. "Stop worrying, I'll be fine. Goodnight! I love you..."

"Of course, I'm going to worry. My little girl is having a baby! And I know just how important this baby is to you." Marie leaned forward and kissed Cáel on her forehead. "I love you too, darling. Goodnight."

***

Cáel wished Michael would kiss her.

Oh, it's such a bad idea! Of course it is. There are so many reasons why it is, Cáel rationalized in her mind. For one, *I've just met him, like, a few hours ago. Secondly, he's in the army, and I'm hardly a supporter of long-distance relationships. Thirdly, I've just come out of a ten year serious relationship which ended badly, leaving me devastated and miserable. A hot one night stand, yes, it would definitely help my brittle self-esteem, but that's not me.*

Besides, it's hardly sensible to replace one long term boyfriend promptly with a hot Asian guy who was incredibly sexy. Yes, a romantic interlude was tempting, but this was hardly the time for seeking new romance, I can do without complicating my...

Michael's lips were on hers. He was kissing her. Cáel's thoughts and warnings were discarded immediately as she felt herself responding to him. Soon, they were kissing passionately. Cáel could feel his tongue deep in her mouth, coaxing her into surrender. Michael held her face in his warm hands, his lips were insistent on hers, both soft and hard at the same time. Perspiration broke out of Cáel's temples as carnal heat rose up from deep below, all the way to her lips.

Cáel woke from the dream with an involuntary jerk. For a few seconds she was lost, with no sense of time and place, feeling as if she was back in time, re-experiencing the event instead of just recalling a memory. The dream of her first kiss with Michael was so intense that she had lived it all over again, unable to fully recognize it as reminiscence.

Slowly, she made sense of where she was and what had happened. She was in real time, and there was no Michael, only a rancid taste of his betrayal. She was in Fort Lauderdale, in her mother's house, in her old room, and Myra was sleeping next to her.

She fumbled for the small watch on her nightstand. It was two o'clock in the morning. She lay back on her pillow and stared out the window. They curtain was aside and bright moonlight streamed into the room, illuminating the floor next to the window. Her head felt clear and she marveled at the tenacity of the human body and brain. Her memories were coming back clearly and quickly now, and she could understand her world much better as compared to the first two days when she'd gotten discharged from University Medical Center.

Cáel went over the day in her mind. It was an ocean of Michael's memories, and how ever she tried not getting sucked into them, they kept coming back every time she closed her eyes. She realized she had to deal with them; her latent memory channels won't spare her, now that they were stronger and bolder.

Now, in the quiet of the night, her brain refreshed from the sleep, she went over what she remembered of her love story with Michael. Her mind brought forward the first time they had made love.

It had been their second day together. Michael had been at Cáel's door at ten o'clock in the morning, red roses in his hands. Deciding that the morning was too beautiful to do anything that wasn't outdoors, they had driven to a beach a few miles away from the main strip, a secluded little spot where no one disturbed them.

She and Michael had spent the day on the

beach. They had talked all day, interrupting their conversation only to swim, read, and nap. They had kissed and caressed on the sand, until they could bear it no more. Then they had gone back to Cáel's apartment, unable to keep their hand off each other any longer.

Michael had his arms around her, pulling her shorts down even before she had closed the apartment door, and untied her bikini top, kissing her all the while. They only time their lips parted from each other was when Cáel had yanked his tee-shirt over his head. They were on the floor in the living room in no time, their bodies rubbing and uniting as they had made urgent love on the rug in the late afternoon glow.

Tired, they had dozed off in each other's arms. When they woke up, it had been dark outside. Michael had picked Cáel up in his arms and carried her to the bed. There he had made slow, passionate love to her all over again, this time taking his time, admiring her naked beauty, kissing and teasing her salty breasts until she was quivering like a feather. Michael was a skilled lover, and by the time they were through, Cáel was both satiated and moaning for more.

They hadn't slept at all that night, and after that night, it had been a fast roller coaster ride. Cáel had lost all awareness of the world, completely lost in the chemistry that she and Michael shared. She had forgotten her family, work, and studies for those ten days they had been together. Her apartment had become their universe, and they spent every waking moment together, going out only to eat.

They understood that there are some natural laws that govern the sexual journey of two individuals, and that there was no controlling or twisting these laws. They knew that their existed a special magnet between then, pulling them into dizzying depths of love. The night before Michael was to leave they had admitted to each other that they were madly in love.

Michael had asked Cáel to be his girlfriend and wait for him to return from his tour to Afghanistan. She had readily agreed.

Michael left for Afghanistan in October. A chain of regular letters and emails began between them, strengthening their love for each other. Meanwhile, Cáel joined her new job, doing well in the field. By the time Michael was back, it was March and Cáel was moving to Las Vegas on promotion. Michael helped her with her packing, and he settled in Lubbock, Texas, his hometown, and his home base.

Cáel took Michael to meet her family, and they liked him instantly. She and Michael continued seeing each other regularly over the next few months. She visited him once a month in Lubbock, and the couple of times she couldn't, Michael had come to Las Vegas to be with her.

Until she got pregnant. She just couldn't

remember what had happened after that? Did they never meet again? Were they not in touch at all? Her brains own defense mechanism had blocked out what she presumed was the most painful part of her dying relationship with Michael.

***

Cáel strung one delicate crystal of memory after another into the thread of fragmented time as memories returned to her mind, finding their old resting places in the curbs and corners of her consciousness, happy to be back in the clear order of occurrence, where they belonged.

CHAPTER 18

Going over their love story, Cáel suddenly remembered that she had stored a carton of letters in her mom's attic, when she had vacated her apartment, to move to Las Vegas. When the first stream of sunlight lit her bedroom window, she got out of bed, leaving Myra sleeping, and went straight to the attic of the house.

Climbing into the musty, moth-ridden place, Cáel sifted through piles and piles of old stuff. It was a bombardment of memories from her teen years. There were pictures of her and her friends dressed in the grungy attire of the late nineties, old gifts from her sisters that she had stashed away, hoping to come back to them and indulge in the happy memories, neatly folded gift wrapping papers reminiscent of gifts of sheer stockings and erotic letters by old long-forgotten boyfriends.

Cáel smiled at each of these items, wiping the

dust off them and feeling the weight of past on her fingers. But she didn't linger too long on them because she was looking for something in particular. She was searching for that carton of memories of Michael.

She found the carton lying at one end of the outside wall, still taped up and intact. She leaned toward it and pulled it closer, removing the duct-tape and dust. In the carton lay dozens of cards and letters that had been written to her by Michael. She pulled them all out, a thick bundle, and went through them one by one.

They were letters of love and longing, so consistent in their potent adoration, that they left Cáel unfurled. Michael had written a letter every day to her. Some days, the letter had been just, 'I'm tired, and I love you' and other days, the letter was an eleven page pledge of devotion. Some envelopes had three, four letters in them, dated differently, but probably posted together.

Losing all her bitterness into the oblivion of loving memories triggered by the letters and cards, Cáel emerged anew. She was convinced that someone who could so unfailingly send his love to her every single day from a ravaged warzone halfway across the world could not have been a cad or a coward. She was sure now, despite her broken recollections, that their love had been real. She was certain, despite Christopher and Amanda telling her otherwise, that Michael had really wanted to be with her.

Cáel heard footsteps behind her. It was Marie, her mother.

"Honey, what are you doing up here so early?"

"Ma, I can't get a grip on whatever's happened with Michael. Here, take a look at these letters, from when he was away in Afghanistan," Cáel waved the letters toward her mother. "He honestly, really, truly loved me, Ma. It didn't make any sense. He wouldn't have deserted me. It wasn't in his nature."

Marie walked up to Cáel and sat down heavily on a stool. She was thoughtful for a minute, and then she said, "I can totally understand where this is coming from, because he appeared to be a gentleman. Plus, if things had really gone irreversibly sour between you two, you would've confided in me about it."

"Maybe I believed he would come back eventually," Cáel reasoned, her brows knitted together, trying to recall something of what had happened after the news of her pregnancy.

"Maybe," answered Marie, echoing Cáel's thoughts.

"We'll never know now, it's so tragic!" Cáel cried, frustrated at the futility of the conversation, knowing she'll never know everything because Michael was dead.

"Honey, do you really need to? Sometimes

things happen in life which our totally out of your control. You cannot control everything! What you actually need is to let go. You have to move on, Cáel. He's gone, and you still have your life."

"Funny, that's exactly what Chris said to me last night."

"Well, he was right. What did he say to you?"

"He said I could move on, with someone new, that I'm free now."

"Did he mean himself? I have a feeling his feelings for you are more than friendly," Marie questioned in a voice that said, 'I've seen it all.'

"He kissed me," Cáel admitted to her mother. "I don't know, Ma, and it's all confusing. Isn't it a bit too early to be seeing someone new?"

"Maybe that's what you need right now; someone new to sweep you off your feet.

Having a man in the house isn't so bad when you have a baby to bring up."

"It didn't help you, Ma. What help was Dad to you?"

"Sweetheart, you have to understand I was brought up in a different world. I was taught to expect very little from life."

Cáel closed her eyes and saw her mother, in the prime of her life, scrubbing a sooty kitchen, taking care of the young children, saving dimes to buy a junior prom dress for Sarah, while her husband is absent from their lives.

"And you have to understand how much I loved your father. It was good for a while. Then it just died out. I made my choices in my life, as we all must, and I'm at peace with them. The question for you is what are your choices? What do you believe you deserve in your life?"

It was hard for Cáel to imagine a life without Michael in it. Even just to think that she would never hear his cajoling voice in her ears, or feel his strong arms around her, was scary. She thought of Christopher's warm, seductively smooth voice saying, "He's gone now, Cáel. And you... you can be free. You can fall in love again. Take another love. Marry somebody else... Think about it."

"It isn't so bad to allow someone to care for you, Cáel."
"I agree with you, Ma, but right now, until I remember every bit of what exactly happened with Michael, I cannot start the process of letting go," she said. "I should get back tomorrow, I need to see my doctor."

"You do what you have to do, Cáel. Get your affairs in order. I have full faith in your capability in taking care of your business, Marie said sternly. "By the time the baby comes, you should've sorted your problems, or I'll be very disappointed in you!"

CHAPTER 19

Cáel's goodbye to her family was emotional. Her mother wanted her to stay put in Fort Lauderdale, while Myra insisted she'd come and live with her in Vegas, at least to see her through her pregnancy. She tearfully turned down their generous offers, promising them she'll take good care of herself.

The flight back to Las Vegas gave her time to think and answer the questions running around in her head. Throughout the flight she mulled, twisted, and probed the thoughts and memories that were locked away somewhere in the deep recesses of her brain. She desperately tried to yank them out into the sunlight, where she could make a head and tail of them, pushing her cerebral capacity to remember what happened after she got pregnant.

She decided the only way she would remember things is if someone jogged her memory with her. She made a mental note to call Amanda as soon as possible and get together with her.

Soon she was at McCarran Airport; Cáel collected her luggage, feeling growing hunger pangs. She marveled at how frequently she was getting hungry with the baby growing inside. She thought back on all the advice she had got from her mother on taking care of her eating habits and berated herself for being careless, in spite of being pregnant, Cáel quickly ordered a lunch of a fish sandwich and a large salad.

From the airport, Cáel went straight to the University Medical Center to see her psychologist, Dr. Monica Sutherland. She had called and set up an appointment, knowing well how busy the doctor was, and she was ushered into her office without any wastage of time.

The doctor was going through Cáel's file which lay open on her desk.

"How are you, Cáel?" Dr. Sutherland greeted her. "How was your visit back home?"

"It was very fruitful and relaxing, thanks, Doctor," Cáel replied with a smile.

"You're back much earlier than I expected though, our next appointment was after four days? Is everything okay?" Dr. Sutherland questioned her.

"I don't know if everything is okay. I'm very confused, Doctor."

Dr. Sutherland nodded understandingly.

"I told you so. This will be a confusing time for you, Cáel. It'll be good for you to flush out the peripheral thoughts and concentrate on your baby. Pushing yourself to regain memory is only going to add to the stress of post-trauma."

"I've been able to recall a lot of my life in the last week, and that way, I stand on much firmer ground than I did when I'd been discharged from here."

"I can see that, Cáel. You look more self-assured," the doctor agreed. "But you tell me you're confused?" she asked with a smile.

"I just cannot recall the span of time from my breakup with Michael to my accident."

"Well, Cáel, there is no possible way to control how your brain will unfold and churn out the inexhaustible amounts of data it has stored away in its creases. You can't possibly control or predict this. Your brain is going to follow its own pattern in reminiscing. The more you pressurize yourself into remembering episodes, the more they'll play hide and seek, especially if these particular memories were painful or traumatic for you."

"I understand, but I'm sure there is something important that I'm missing, there's something that isn't quite adding up," Cáel stressed.

"What do you mean?"

"I mean, I know Michael bailed out on me and the baby, but there's a little voice in my head that's saying, it isn't like that, look deeper. When I was home at Fort Lauderdale, I saw our old photos and letters, and they were full of deep love and affection. I find it hard to believe he would desert me! There's something missing in the whole picture. I refuse to believe we just broke off and then he never tried contacting me, knowing very well I was carrying his baby!"

"Cáel, if you're so sure of it, you need to go backward in your memories and connect the dots. The pieces will come together, I assure you. Meanwhile, don't forget to take all the necessary care in your pregnancy. Have you seen your doctor? You must be up for an ultrasound examination this month?

Cáel nodded. "I'm having it done tomorrow."

"Check up on the prenatal classes that our family resource center, Baby-Steps, offers for expecting mothers. They'll help. Do you know the building? It's a block away, a five minute walk."

***

Cáel left the psychologist's office, and decided to walk it to 'Baby-Steps,' the UMC Family Resource Center.

She went up to the reception desk and gave her name to the clerk.

"I'd like to sign up for your childbirth classes, please," Cáel specified.

"Just a second, Ma'am, are you a Baby-Steps patient?"

"I am."

"May I have your name, please?" The clerk

queried.

"Cáel Darcie."

The clerk typed in the name, and scrutinized the computer screen in front of her. Then her brow furrowed.

"Ma'am, you've already signed up for the class. Your name is fed into our system."

"I have? When?" Cáel asked, puzzled, presuming she might've signed up before her injury.

"You gave your name on the tenth of January," the clerk read out from her records, "You signed up along with your childbirth partner, Michael Chan. Yes, I remember you both. I was on duty that morning."

Cáel was amazed to hear Michael's name.

"Let me have a look."

Cáel peered in at the screen to confirm whether what she'd just heard was true or not. Michael's name was right there, alongside her name. January tenth. It was the day Michael had got shot!

A scene flashed before her eyes. She was in the same lobby, and Michael was entering from the glass doors, giving a tentative smile to Cáel. He had walked up to the desk and greeted her.

"I'm here."

"I'm not so sure about this…" Cáel had replied.

"Let's just sign up now and we'll talk later, okay?"

Cáel snapped out of her reverie. The clerk was looking at her strangely, as though she was a bit loony.

"Uh, okay, thanks. I'll attend the next class."

Cáel handed her the form and rushed out of the door.

***

She stepped out into the sunshine, totally baffled. She wondered what Mike was doing in the hospital with her? Why was he signing up for the class? He didn't want to have anything to do with her or the baby. She knew he had been in Las Vegas, and they had met up in the evening, which had turned out catastrophically. But no one told her he had been with her for the classes. She thought back on her recollection. Michael had looked meek, almost apologetic.

He had wanted to be here! That's the missing piece.

A part of her wondered why Christopher hadn't mentioned anything about it. Maybe he didn't know of it, she reasoned. Whatever it was, there was more to things than what she understood.

Cáel reached home, thinking about what she had learned. She felt tired, the flight had been long, and she was mentally exhausted trying to grasp the cloudy events of her immediate past. She called Amanda.

"Hey Mindy, I'm back!"

"Cáel, babe! I was wondering if you've decided to settle yourself in that cute cottage with mommy! In the last few days, there's been no news from you! How are you, how was your visit, and how is everyone at home?" Amanda squealed into the phone, happy to hear from her. Fort Lauderdale was Amanda's hometown too, and she wanted to hear more about it. "Why don't we meet up in the night? Dinner?"

Cáel, always infected by her quirky friend's exuberance, found herself grinning into the phone.

"Sure, you read my mind. I'll come over tonight. There's a lot to tell you."

"Cool, but don't drive out yourself. Take a cab."

CHAPTER 20

"Hey, don't you have your ultrasound exam tomorrow?" Amanda asked with a twinkle in her eye.

They had just finished a dinner of French casserole and grilled chicken, and had moved to the famous red couch in the living room of Amanda's apartment. Neil Diamond crooned over the night radio, and Amanda was almost through with her bottle of wine.

Cáel smiled at the thought. "Yes, and I'm rather excited and apprehensive all at the same time. I hope all is fine with the baby, you know... with my injury and everything."

"Everything's fine, they've examined the baby many times when you were in coma. You'll know the sex of the baby, too! Text me immediately."

"I'll certainly do that! Oh, I must tell you

about my trip back home."

Cáel filled her in with the happenings at Fort Lauderdale; Amanda had been waiting to hear about it all and was excited.

***

"Chris kissed you?"

Amanda's big kohl-lined eyes were wide open. So was her mouth, such that together they gave her the expression of a struck bird; a canary, to be more precise, because she wore a flowing canary yellow dress.

"I knew it! I knew he had a crush on you!" she chimed, animated.

"Oh, don't read so much into it, it was a spur-of-the-moment thing." Cáel tried to make slight of it. She had felt a seed of doubt settling in regarding Christopher, since the afternoon at UMC. Cáel was an extremely straight-forward person, and she did not like it when facts were kept from her.

"Oh, don't you 'spur-of-the-moment' this," Amanda persisted. "He's had the hots for you since he started hanging out with us. Why else would he be there for you all the time?"

Cáel thought about that and suddenly asked Amanda, "When was that?"

"What?" Amanda grimaced.

"When did we start to hang out together — Chris and I? For the life of me, I can't remember!"

"Hmm, of course you don't remember," Amanda nodded and then knitted her brow together in concentration. "It was... sometime in November, after you got pregnant."

"You mean, right after Mike and I broke up?"
"Yeah, actually that's right."

"Don't you think that's a bit strange? Why would I have anything to do with Mike's best friend, if I was trying to move forward after the breakup? I would want to be miles away from anything that had something to do with Mike."

"Oh, things aren't always that simple, Cáel. You were in a state of shock for a bit there. You never expected this from Mike. Actually, you were sort of using Chris to get back at Mike. At least that's how it started out. But Chris always stuck up for you. Slowly Chris made his place in our hearts by always being there for you."

Cáel frowned.

"Tell me everything from the beginning. When did we meet Chris?"

"Okay," Amanda rolled her eyes. Sighing, she said, "It is a long story. You knew Chris through Mike. Chris was stationed here after his Afghanistan deputation and Mike always caught up with him when he was here to see you. They were close friends. When Mike denied the baby and asked you to get an abortion, Chris and Mike had a huge row about it. Chris had really let Mike have it. He obviously cared about you!

"You were going for your first doctor's appointment the next day. Chris went with you, and Mike flew back to Lubbock. That's how Chris got close to you and took care of you in the initial months."

Cáel had a flash of Christopher cooking for her, in his kitchen, slowly stirring a pot of chicken stew, while talking to Cáel at the same time. Amanda was there too, along with her awful boyfriend, Dylan. Dylan was buttering rolls of bread, while Amanda was mixing a green salad. All of them were in animated conversation about Michael, because Christopher had just told them he was coming to Vegas for New Year's. Amanda was suggesting to Cáel that they dress up and go to the same New Year's bash, where Michael was going to be with Christopher.

Coming out of the flashback, Cáel turned to Amanda.

"I just remembered something, Mindy. Did Mike come back here for New Year's?"

"Yes, he did. He, heh… we really got back at him that night," Amanda giggled. "We decided to crash the same party. That was the first time he saw you after your breakup. There he was, hanging out with Chris next to the bar, when you had walked in looking stunning, as usual. He was zapped and speechless for a while, like he'd seen a ghost. He couldn't keep his eyes off you, and Chris wouldn't let him approach you, that was part of the plan."

Now Cáel remembered that party. She closed her eyes and saw herself there, in the nightclub, dressed in a deep-necked, wine-colored knee-length dress. It flared at the bottom and swung around her legs seductively as she danced. She could see Michael from the corner of her eye. He looked at her unblinking, and he never once looked away. His gaze had given her goose bumps. It had taken every ounce of her self-control to not go up to him.

"...You had flirted with every gorgeous hunk in the party and completely ignored him!" Amanda was talking, pulling Cáel out of her reverie.

"Ignored him? We did not speak at all?" Cáel queried.

"No, we started dancing on the floor. He appeared to have had a long argument with Chris, next to the bar, and then he just left. We got together with Chris then, and he told us how surprised he was to see Cáel, the poor guy! How we laughed about it!"

Cáel honestly did not see it as very funny now,

and she inwardly wished she hadn't played these games with Michael, who most certainly would've been tortured that night. I would've certainly been tortured, thought Cáel, if I was watching the love of my life and mother of my child in every John Doe's arms.

Wait a minute, Cáel reasoned in her head. Did I just call myself the love of his life? Am I feeling bad for him? Am I sorry I was teasing him? How can I sympathize with him? Unless... I believed we still loved each other. He still loved me! He wanted to be back together!

Cáel couldn't remember instances or any conversation that could confirm this gut feeling, but she was sure that this was the missing piece — Michael had realized his mistake and he had wanted to get back together. The fact that he had signed up for prenatal classes with her was pointing toward that. She decided to bring it up with Amanda.

"You're not going to believe what I learned today, Mindy. Michael had signed up for childbirth classes along with me on tenth of January."

"Huh? That's the day he... right?"

"Yeah, I didn't know this, and no one told me about it. Strange, isn't it?"

"That he signed up for something like that? Yeah, strange," Amanda agreed, thoughtful.

"Mindy, what happened after New Year's? Did I meet him again, in your knowledge?"

"I'm not sure about that. Something was up, because Chris was with you a lot after that. I was having trouble keeping my relationship with Dylan afloat; all my energy was concentrated there. You and I weren't seeing each other too often those days. Oh, but you know what — you came to know Mike was getting married to some Chinese girl."

A memory of Christopher jarred her just then. It was the same flashback Cáel had had when she had met Christopher first time in Amanda's home, a week ago, after her discharge from UMC.

In the memory, she was standing next to him in a kitchen. Christopher had been cooking spaghetti in a reddish sauce. There was a sense of sadness in the memory, and Cáel felt the anxiety of that evening scene in her body. A shiver ran through her.

Now she remembered the scene fully. It was the evening of the first of January, right after the New Year's party. Christopher had just told her Michael was getting married. Cáel recalled the exchange.

"What?"

"Yeah, that's what he said, Cáel. There's a Chinese chick. His folks like her a lot."

"What about him? Does he like her too?"

Cáel looked back and felt her pain from that day plummet through her consciousness. It brought tears to her eyes. Cáel's heart had been crushed that night in Christopher's kitchen, because till then, she had still been unknowingly harboring some hope to get back with Michael.

Cáel shook away the melancholy that threatened to blanket her and turned her attention to Amanda, who was talking.
"...Yeah, Chris told you. You were mad! You actually planned to meet him and give him something that would make him impotent."

"Is there such a thing?"

"Apparently, yeah, you got it from a Chinese store. Ironic, ain't it?"

Cáel laughed, despite herself.

CHAPTER 21

Cáel was disturbed.

She ran her hands through her hair, messaging her aching head, and slumped back into the sofa in her living room, where she had been sitting since she got back from Amanda's place. The whole place was dark, it was way past midnight, but she was too uneasy to sleep.

Her discoveries — Michael's presence at UMC the day he died and the rush of memories that had assaulted her throughout her evening with Amanda — had left her distressed and restless.

"I have to get to the bottom of all this!" she thought to herself. Her mind went back to the New Year's party. She could picture Michael standing next to Christopher, her mind's eye zooming in to his face; his eyes. What she saw in them was hurt.

Cáel squirmed inside. She got up, put on a low light, and started pacing the room. Her mind went over the details of what she had remembered, what Amanda had revealed, trying to get the events in the correct order of sequence.

Michael had broken up with her. After that, the next time she had seen him was at New Year's, by that time she'd also learned through Christopher that Michael had been seeing an Asian chick.

But, definitely she had seen Michael again, because he had signed up for the childbirth classes with her. This mystery befuddled her. Obviously he had at some point got back in touch with her and had wanted to be a part of her life. Now the question was, why hadn't Christopher told her about this? It wasn't possible he didn't know. He had to know! Was Christopher keeping things from her? Was he taking advantage of her loss of memory?

These were some of the question floating in Cáel's head. A slow trickle of distrust crept into her understanding of Christopher. She couldn't rely on him. There had to be another way of finding out what communication transpired between Michael and her after the New Year's party.

Michael had communicated with her. How? Cáel thought of her cell phone. There would be records of all her calls in there. But her phone was in police custody. She made a mental note to call the detective in charge in the morning. Where else could she find the answers?

Suddenly Cáel thought of Michael's laptop that she had brought back from Lubbock. She had not had time to go through it since she'd come back. She rushed into her bedroom and opened the locked suitcase lying in one corner. She pulled out the laptop and sat down on her bed with it in her lap. She switched it on swiftly, plugging the battery cable into an electric socket.

Cáel tried accessing his email inbox, but it was protected with a password and she had no idea what it was. She tried 'Afghanistan.' It wasn't accepted. She tried it spelled backward. It didn't work. She then typed the number of his platoon, his course number, his birthday, his birthplace in China, his favorite band… nothing worked. The inbox was locked and staring back at her Cáel pressed hard against her latent memory. She had a vague recollection that she had known Michael's password, he had shared it with her, and it had something to do with his army detail. Frustrated, she was about to give up, when she saw Michael's dog tags lying in the suitcase, on top of other little things she had brought along from Lubbock.

Cáel jumped off the bed and grabbed the metal plates. Michael's service number was engraved on them. She typed it out in the space next to 'password' on the computer-screen.

It didn't work.

She shut her eyes tight and let out a deep sigh. She glared at the tiny empty space next to 'password.' Then she typed out Michael's service-number backward, and clicked on, 'sign-in.'

The screen vanished for a couple of seconds, and when it was back, Cáel was in Michael's e-mail inbox.

CHAPTER 22

"Yes!" Cáel screamed out in elation.

"Talk to me, Mike, talk to me!" She whispered as she scrolled down the list of emails.

She stopped when she found a thread of e-chat between Christopher and Michael dated early January, in fact it was third of January. She clicked it open, her fingers trembling. It read:

> Michael: Hey Chris, so, did you speak to Cáel at all? I know she's mad at me, but since you've been around her, maybe she'll listen to you, you know?
>
> Christopher: No, man, I haven't met her at all these last few days.
>
> Michael: You know where she lives, dude. Go meet her and plead my case.

Christopher: I don't know, man, I have nothing to do with her. I can't drop in just like that. We barely know each other. Plus, I think she's already seeing another guy.

Michael: Damn it! I just want to be a part of my baby's life, that's all!

Christopher: Hey, why don't you just forget about this chapter of your young life, and move on with Lily. She's hot, sexy, and Chinese. Go for it!

Michael: I don't love Lily. It's my folks who love her. To tell you the truth, I can't get Cáel off my mind. She's still got my heart.

Christopher: When did you become such a sucker, dude?

Cáel did not have to read more to know what had happened. She was stunned. Christopher had been playing a game with her all this time. She felt as though the earth had abruptly shifted and vanished below her feet.

Christopher had driven a wedge through the crack that had appeared in her relationship with Michael. She wondered at how long he had been at it? Maybe he was the one who pressurized Michael into abandoning his unborn child?

She also wondered about his motives. What could have prompted him to backstab his own best friend? Was he even worth calling a friend? Was it her fault? Was she the reason? Despair and sadness surrounded her, and then it gave way to seething hatred for Christopher Bush.

She thought back of her previous recollection of dinner at Christopher's house, when he had told her about Michael seeing a Chinese girl.

He had told her that they might be getting married soon. She felt nauseous at the thought, exactly as how she'd felt at that time in her recollection.

Suddenly, Cáel had another flashback.

She's was in a theatre. There was a live show going on at the center of the huge auditorium. She was with Christopher. On her other side sat Amanda and a new date that Amanda had brought along, another good looking African American dude, a probable replacement for Dylan. Cáel remembered thinking where Amanda found them — these perfectly shaped and muscled, sexy prototypes of Dylan?

When the show was over, they had walked out together and then parted ways. Christopher was dropping Cáel home. In the car she had brought up the subject of Michael. It had really been bothering her — Michael and the Chinese girlfriend.

Now she recalled the dialogue with Christopher clearly.

"I still cannot believe Michael found someone to replace me in his life so quickly!"

"Doll, why are you torturing yourself so much about it? His parents want him to get married. Forget it!"

"I want to see him. Just once, Chris."

"What? Why?"

"He's been calling me, you know? Since the New Year's party, he's called me every day. I haven't answered his calls. Now I'm thinking I will."

"Why? It's only going to cause you more heartache."

"I want to know what he has to say."

"Look Cáel, you really should stay away from Michael now. I mean it. It's for your own safety."

"What the hell do you mean?"

"Cáel, he's trying to start a great new life with Lily. Guess what's in his way?"

"The baby?"

"Exactly. And he'll do anything to have it out of the way."

"C'mon, Chris, what are you trying to tell me? He can't hurt us! He's not a violent man at all!"

"Cáel, my doll, you have no idea what that guy can do when he's cornered. His feelings for the baby are clear anyway. Why do you want to risk it all? You should just move away and change your name or something."

"I'm not afraid of him."

"You should be. Believe me, there is a dark side to him that you're not even aware of."

Cáel had gone quiet, and pursed her lips grimly. She was then more than determined to give him the liquid she'd bought from a Chinese store on advice from her friends — the one that can make a man impotent.

"I'm going to set up a date with him."

"Well, if you're so determined to do that, please don't do it alone. I'll be with you. In fact, let's meet him at my place. It'll be our turf."

***

Coming out of the flashback, Cáel was shaken up. The reminiscence had left no doubt in her mind about Christopher's dubious stance. He had been playing her all along! And he had had her eating out of her hands! He had been fooling his good friend, Michael, too.

No wonder he did not want her to meet Michael without him present. He was afraid his treachery might come out in the open.

Christopher hated Michael. He was no friend; he only wanted everything that Michael had, including Cáel. In fact, he would've easily killed Michael coldheartedly. All the warmth that he'd showered on Cáel was just pretense, make believe. She could feel a slow anger rising from within her. What a fool she had been!

During all the emotional ups and downs she had been through in the last few days, it had never struck her to ask Christopher why exactly was Michael there in Las Vegas on the tenth of January? And why had they been meeting up? Hadn't they parted ways? What had brought Michael to her?

"I have to be careful now," she cautioned herself.

She tried her best to remember how she and Michael met that fateful night and what had happened before Michael got shot, but nothing came out of her wayward memory bank. She was now sure that there was more to things than what met the eye, as far as Michael's death was concerned.

I should talk to Detective Davis. I should try and talk to that guy Russell too, she decided, thinking of Christopher's roommate, whose gun had fired and killed Michael.

Cáel lay back on the pillows and tried to calm down. As the first ray of the sun hit her window, she went into a fitful disturbed sleep.

CHAPTER 23

Cáel woke up with a start. It was bright and sunny outside, and the phone was ringing. Groggily, she padded up to the landline and squinted at the number flashing in the caller-ID.

It was Christopher.

She was wide awake and alert now. She picked up the receiver cautiously.

"Hello?"

"Cáel, doll, its Chris," Christopher's even voice reached Cáel's ear.

"Hey, uh-hi," Cáel managed to say, her heart racing and the rush of blood throbbing into her head.

"Hey, are you okay? You sound strange," Christopher asked.

"I-I'm fine, absolutely fine."

"Good, when did you get back from your mom's? You didn't call?"

"Umm, I came yesterday... uh, it was a busy day," Cáel tried to bring normalcy in her voice, but an acute sense of danger made her rather afraid.

"Okay... so, I called to ask if you want me to come along for your ultrasound today."

Cáel did not want Chris around until she could get a grip on her raging emotions.

"No, Chris," she replied. "I think I'll get this done on my own."

"Are you sure? Because I can take the rest of the day off, you know."

"I'm pretty sure. Umm, why don't I meet up with you later in the day or something?"

"Yeah, sure thing, Cáel, I missed you."

Cáel winced. She thought of the kiss and bile rose from her stomach. Swallowing hard, she said bye and hung up.

***

Sitting in her Ob-Gyn's office waiting room, Cáel couldn't help but think of Michael. In the last two weeks she had gone from loving to hating, back to loving him all over again. She reflected on how strangely everything had turned out. Last year this time, she would've never imagined life could take such a strange turn.

"Miss Cáel Darcie?" It was a young spectacled assistant, reading out from a clipboard in her arm.

"That would be me."

"You're up next for the ultrasound. Please

follow me."

Cáel got up and did that. She entered a dark room which was lit only by the light of the ultrasound imaging screen. The assistant told her to lie down.

Lying on the cold bed, her belly exposed, she realized that until now, she hadn't actually given a proper thought to this particular test. It was an important milestone in her pregnancy. Today she was to learn if her baby is perfectly developed, competent to live his life healthy, and whether it's a boy or a girl.

Cáel was very, very nervous. Tears stung her eyes and she wished her mother was with her. She rebuked herself for not being more careful in her pregnancy. Now Cáel felt her heart was going to come out of her chest and the wait seemed interminable. She found herself praying that everything goes fine.

Finally, her radiologist walked in.

"Hey there, how are you doing?" The doctor greeted her as if lying there, all cold and nervous, was the most natural thing in the world. "You're nervous. Don't worry, just try and relax."

Cáel rolled her eyes and flinched as the doctor poured cold jelly on her belly and placed his gadget on her, his eyes trained to the screen. The screen was now alive with an image. It was her uterus and there was a perfect little being in there. It was moving, and kicking. The doctor zoomed on the upper body, and Cáel saw a flutter. It was a steady flutter. The heartbeat!

She stared at it. Wow, that's my baby!

"The baby's doing well, Cáel. He looks good, he has a strong, steady heartbeat."

"He? It's a boy?" Cáel couldn't believe she had just learned she was having a boy!

"Yeah, it's a boy! Congratulations!"

She turned to the screen, tears of excitement and relief at her baby's well-being running down her face. She could see the baby's spine and head. Her heart skipped a beat. He wasn't a shadow, or a skeleton. He was real — her son. He was growing and he was beautiful.

The doctor checked for other parameters like heart rate, uterus, cervix length, brain, etcetera, but Cáel was glued to the moving image on the screen. It was a wonderful moment and she wished she wasn't alone. She wished Michael was with her.

CHAPTER 24

Cáel messaged Amanda, her mother, and her sisters about the exam results as soon as she reached home. Calls started coming in almost immediately. She kept them short, because she wanted to call Michael's parents, Shen and Li Juan, as early as possible. She had been talking to them almost every day since she'd come back from Lubbock and eagerly wanted to give them the news. She dialed their number, wishing she could've told them about her baby boy in person.

"Hello, Mr. Chan, its Cáel."

"Cáel, how are you? How did the exam go?" Shen and Li Juan Chan were waiting as keenly for the results of the exam as Cáel.

"The baby's doing well, Mr. Chan. And guess what? It's a boy!"

"Cáel, that's great news! Wait till Li Juan hears

this, haha!"

Shen Chan was obviously ecstatic to hear the sex of the baby. Cáel laughed along with him, happy to sense their happiness.

"Well, you convey the news to her and I'll talk to you soon!"

"All right, bye Cáel. Take care of yourself."

She hung up and straight away her mind turned to the pressing matter of her cell phone. She rummaged through her bag for Detective Davis' business card and called his office number.

He answered the phone on its second jingle.

"Detective Davis."

"Hello, Detective, I'm Cáel Darcie. We met a couple of weeks ago, uh, on the Michael Chan case."

"Yes, of course. How are you and how may I help you?"

"Detective, I was wondering if you could give me some sort of contact number for Russell White, the accused in the case?"

"I think I should be able to. Hang on; let me look for the file."

The detective was quiet for a minute, and then he said, "His current address is Afghanistan. He's out on deployment. There is no way to really call him. What's going on?"

"Detective, I think there's something fishy about the whole thing. Is it possible to reopen the case?"

"Not unless you have new incriminating evidence."

"I don't. It's just a hunch right now. That's why I just wanted to speak with Russell. I can't remember the evening; I was hoping he would be able to jog my memory a little."

"Well, I wish I could help you, but the case is closed. Oh, you should come by and pick up your cell phone from the evidence archive here."

"My cell phone? Yes, I think I'll stop by right away."

***

Cáel put her phone on charge and switched it on.

First, she went over the call logs in January. Sure enough, there had been many calls from Michael, all of them missed calls. Cáel had chosen not to speak with him, except twice.

She sat up. The first call had been received on the morning of the eighth of January, and the second on the tenth of January, the day

Michael had died. She had taken the call and spoken with him. So, they hadn't met by chance that day at Christopher's house, as Christopher had told her and the police. It was a planned meeting. It was the meeting Cáel had spoken to Christopher about in her flashback the previous night.

"Another fact Chris kept from me," Cáel worked out silently.

She started skimming through her text messages on the ninth of January. There was one text from Michael. It said:

> *My flight lands at eight o'clock in the night. I'm staying with Chris. I would like to accompany you to your childbirth class tomorrow. Looking forward...*
>
> **M.**

Cáel ran the equation in her head. "Michael came from Lubbock to Las Vegas on the ninth of January.

We must've spoken to each other on the eighth."

She couldn't recall the conversation. She cursed her memory for the ninth time. "We must've signed sign up for the classes at UMC on tenth. Then we would've met up at Chris's place. That was when he died."

She was stirred out of her thoughts by the ring of the telephone. Before she even reached it, she knew it was Christopher.

"Hello," Cáel said, taking a deep breath and keeping her voice steady.

"Hey, how was the exam?" Christopher asked.

"Hi! Good, great! I'm going to have Michael's son, Chris,"

Cáel replied, bringing some cheer to her tone.

"Wow, that's amazing! Did you tell Michael's

folks?"

"I did, they are thrilled," Cáel marveled at the façade Christopher could pull over his cold, calculating self.

"We should celebrate! Let me take you to a movie and dinner afterward, what do you say?"

"Sure, I'd love to," she answered.

 Let me see how long he keeps this going, she thought to herself.

CHAPTER 25

Christopher picked Cáel up in the evening. Now that the wool that Christopher had pulled over her eyes was off, she was able to see him with an emotionless vision. She stared at his profile during their drive to the movie theatre, hating him more and more with each passing second.

Cáel looked away and checked herself.

I have to get a grip. He's the only one who knows what exactly happened. I have to somehow make him talk about Michael's last visit, and hopefully it will trigger some memory of what had actually taken place. I must try to remember...

The movie was the latest in the 'Bourne' series. It was about an assassin who worked off the radar for the government, and had suffered a memory loss, which led to a series of events endangering his life.

Cáel shook her head. There were similarities in her situation and the main character's and she felt she could completely identify with his actions. *I could actually kill this man sitting next to me right now.*

After the movie ended, Christopher took Cáel to a fine-dining restaurant. After they'd settled, she began to broach the subject with Christopher and feel the waters.

"Hey, tell me something, because I can't remember," she started with a puzzled frown, "Why exactly was Michael in Las Vegas on the tenth of January? It's funny I never really asked you that."

"C'mon Cáel, let's talk about something else. It's your happy day, why do you want to talk about that jerk?"

Cáel boiled inside at the expletive, but kept her exterior calm.

"No, seriously, I want to know."

"What do you want to know? You called him. You wanted to see him."

"And he agreed to come? I thought he wanted nothing to do with me."

"He didn't. You begged him to come and meet you once. You wanted some kind of revenge because you were mighty pissed about him dating another chick."

"Oh? And I suppose I begged him to join childbirth classes with me too?"

Christopher was taken aback at Cáel's words and tone. A strange glint came in his eye as he said, "That happened by chance. He took p-pity on you, because you had cried so much on the phone. You s-s-secretly wanted to get back together with him."

Cáel thought she detected a slight stammer in Christopher's voice. The stammer triggered a memory in her.

It was a scene from the tenth of January, at Baby-Steps. Michael had walked to the receptionist's desk and introduced himself as Cáel's friend and class partner, not the baby's father. That had hurt Cáel. Christopher had been with Michael, lurking behind and he had appeared very uncomfortable. There had been a slight stammer in his voice then.

Coming to think of it now, she realized that Christopher had not left her alone with Michael even for a minute the entire time. She shook off the recollection and looked at Christopher straight in the eye.

"According to my memory, that's not true, Chris."

Chris had gone very quiet now. "What memory Cáel? You don't remember anything, and you don't want to move forward either."

"I won't move forward until I know exactly what took place that night, Chris. And when

I do find out, you'll be the first to know, I promise you that!"

Saying this, Cáel got up and marched out of the restaurant, leaving Chris staring at his napkin.

CHAPTER 26

Cáel was flushed and shaking as she left the restaurant. She was rather terrified and didn't want to be alone. She quickly hailed a cab and gave him Amanda's address. As the taxi moved, she peered back at the entrance of the restaurant, wondering if Christopher intended to follow her.

Seeing no one, she relaxed, sat back in the seat and took stock of things. Her conversation with Christopher hadn't gone as she had hoped. She had wanted to dig around and hear his answers, rather than antagonizing him and walking out.

The cat was now out of the bag and Christopher knew she was onto him. The only thing working for her was that Christopher was an overly confident player and he believed Cáel could come up with nothing. She had to get her act together fast and find some kind of a proof that indicted Christopher.

Soon she was in front of Amanda's door, ringing the bell. She rushed in when Amanda opened it.

"What's going on? Are you okay?" Amanda asked, panicked at the sight of an out-of-breath Cáel.

Cáel spun around and faced her.

"Mindy, we can't trust Chris anymore."

Cáel sat down heavily on the red couch and quickly filled Amanda in on whatever she had discovered and remembered in the last twenty-four hours.

"Oh, my god!" Amanda was open-mouthed and goggle-eyed. "I don't believe it! Poor Michael! He got backstabbed by his own trusted friend!"

"I know! It's awful," Cáel cried tearfully, "I'm sure there's more to Michael's death than we know. We have to get in touch with Russell, but he's gone back to Afghanistan."

"How will you get in touch with him, then?"

"I don't know," Cáel sighed. She dipped her head into her arms, pulling her legs up. "I just don't know, Amanda."

Tears dropped from her eyes and onto her sleeves. Amanda shifted closer to her and held her tight, feeling her friend's pain.

"Forget about talking to Russell. He won't reveal anything relevant, without his lawyer present, anyway," Amanda said, rubbing Cáel's shoulders. "Let's eat something, you haven't had dinner. I have some apple pie and leftover soup."

Amanda went into her kitchen followed by Cáel. Cáel sat down on one of the two chairs, and said, "What do you think Chris had going on in his mind? He's been the catalyst in the complete breakdown on our bond. Maybe Mike and I could have salvaged something out of our relationship had Chris left it alone."

"I don't know what his motives were, but love and jealousy have made people commit heinous crimes throughout history," Amanda commented on Cáel's question as she heated some chicken soup and laid out the bowls.

"Maybe he's psychopathic, and we never saw it. I should dig more into his past."

"Cáel, you're playing with fire. If what you believe of Chris is true, I think you should just stay away from him. I remember Dylan telling me once that last year Chris was obsessing about some chick in his neighborhood, and he chopped her hair off when some guy complimented her blonde hair. After that, she broke up with him. Next day she found her pet dog gutted in her driveway. Rumor has it that Christopher killed that mutt just to teach her a lesson."

"What? That's crazy! How does Dylan know?"

"Apparently, Chris had bragged about it sometime ago, when he was slightly drunk. Cáel, don't get involved in this anymore."

"Michael wanted to get back together and be there for me and the baby. He had no idea his friend was playing him."

"Gosh, that's huge, it's a lot to grasp," Amanda commented, feeling really bad for her friend.

"Yeah, I know. Imagine how close we were to happily-ever-after," Cáel managed a rueful smile. She chewed her slice of pie and thought about the best way to get to the bottom of the mystery.

Amanda and Cáel discussed things and details into the night. Finally, when Cáel felt she could talk no more, Amanda drove her back home.

Changing into Michael's sweatshirt that Cáel had got back from Lubbock, she slipped into bed, utterly dejected, and very lonely. She longed for Michael, and tears sprang into her eyes. She wiped them away and diverted her thoughts to her unborn son.

"Come quickly, my baby, mommy's sad and lonely," she whispered to her son, caressing her stomach, "Don't you worry, everything will be fine, sweetie pie. You're going to have a wonderful life with your mum, and your grannies, and your grandpa, and so many aunts and uncles…"

Talking to her baby, Cáel whispered a small prayer to God, to keep her baby safe and healthy, and she slowly dozed off.

***

Next morning, Cáel woke up and lay in bed

for a long time, not opening her eyes. A part of her wished the morning away. Maybe if the night stretched for a few days, and she slept a long while, she'd wake up and find all of it has gone.

She shook her head at the stupidity of her thoughts and sat up. I won't allow myself to think like a loser, she told herself resolutely and hopped out of bed. Her tummy was growing and visible now, and could notice a change in her walk and body mannerisms. She had become unconsciously more deliberate and careful in her movements — how she sat and got up since her pregnancy had entered the second trimester. Her old agility and quickness had disappeared and given way to slower body language. She liked it, it made her feel good.

Cáel thought about how she would look with a little baby in her arms. I should buy a baby-bag that I can strap around my shoulders and a stroller too. I'll take Mindy and go shopping.

Smiling at the picture in her mind, Cáel felt a flutter of excitement run through her. *Oh, I can't wait for him to come! He'll complete my world, my little angel!*

Feeling reenergized, she made a large, hearty breakfast for herself and took it out to the balcony to eat. Enjoying the early morning sun, she ate her meal, and only then did she finally allow herself to drift back to her problems with Christopher and the huge floating question mark in her head.
She had an idea.

CHAPTER 27

Cáel came back in from the balcony and grabbed some plain sheets of paper from her desk. She poured herself a glass of orange juice, and sat down at the dining table, spreading the blank sheets in front of her.

Slowly and laboriously, she started filling the sheets of paper in her small, neat handwriting. She first wrote down every single bit of recollection she had had since her accident. Then she started to write whatever she had learnt from various sources; Amanda, her mother and sisters, Christopher, the clerk at Baby-Steps. She put down one piece of information on one sheet, and by the time she was through, there were almost thirty sheets lying spread on the table.

Her telephone rang. She ignored it and it went into voice-mail. Christopher's voice boomed into the speaker, jolting Cáel out of her skin.

"Cáel, pick up the phone. I know you're there. Please, can we just talk?"

Cáel pursed her lips and let the line go dead. Then she gathered the papers lying in front of her and went into the bedroom. One by one, she pasted all of the sheets on the wall, making a collage of all her memories, in order of their occurrence in time. She divided them into headings of 'Love,' 'Pregnancy,' and 'Cold-hearted.'

Under 'Love,' she stuck pages of her love affair with Michael right from Fort Lauderdale days to the news of her pregnancy. Under 'Pregnancy,' she pasted memories of her breakup with Michael and her friendship with Christopher. In 'Cold hearted,' she stuck the memories of all the tiny acts of betrayal that Christopher had committed, combined with what she'd got to know of Michael's efforts to get back into her life.

Having created a flow chart of the events of

the last few months, Cáel stood back and studied them for a long time, hoping that the clear vision of events in front of her would help her remember the key elements that were missing from the picture.

After an hour, she popped her prenatal vitamins and went for a long shower. She dipped herself into warm water scented with Michael's bathing salts and lotions, and allowed herself to be washed in his memories, feeling his presence next to her.

Cáel spent the whole day at home, wanting to shut the world out and revitalize herself, wanting to cleanse herself of all the conflicting confusion and mentally conditioning her being to take on the stress with an astute heart. Our baby deserves to know the truth — the truth about what happened to his father.

***

The next morning, her phone rang and woke her up. Once again Christopher's voice messaging system.

"Cáel, for god's sake, call me back when you get this. Where are you? Are you all right?"

Cáel let out her breath, which she had been holding, as she had heard the message. She wasn't sure if she wanted to speak with Christopher ever again. Not as of now, anyway, she confirmed to herself.

She glanced at the wall in her front of her. The wall of papers stared back at her. She got up and scrutinized every piece of paper on the wall, and then went to the kitchen to fix herself a good breakfast.

She decided she wanted to spend the next couple of days in solitude, at home. She did not want to talk to or see anybody until she had some answers. She spent the day and her time eating healthy, doing her light pregnancy exercises, watching her favorite movies, and brainstorming over her memory wall.

Amanda called to check on her, but she ignored the call. She only took the call that came from her mother, assuring her she was doing well and in great spirits, and went back to working on her memory wall.

As Cáel went over the note on her conversation with Detective Davis, she suddenly remembered that a while ago, she had met a detective from Las Vegas police department who worked murder cases.

It was a broken memory from work. She worked as relations manager for her Airline, and the detective had needed a last minute extra ticket for his little daughter, who was traveling with him. The economy seats in the flight had been full, and Cáel had pulled a few strings and got them seats in executive class, which were reserved only for VIPs, as per the Airline rules.

The detective had been extremely thankful, and had given Cáel his business card saying that if she ever needed police help, she should call him.

Cáel was amazed that she remembered something so trivial from a forgotten life and rushed to her desk. She opened the drawers and rummaged through all the business cards she had. At last, she found one by the name, 'Detective Nathan Arnold.' She picked up her phone and dialed the number. It was answered almost instantly.

"Detective Arnold," a crisp voice came on the line.

"Hi, Detective, my name is Cáel Darcie, I wonder if you remember me? We met at the Delta Airlines counter a while ago. I helped you out with your tickets."

"Aah, yes, of course, I remember. You were the pretty manager who seemed to know all the right people! How are you doing?"

"I'm well, detective, how are you and your beautiful little girl? Alice, if I'm not mistaken?"

"You're right; you have a good memory too, along with good PR skills. So, what gives? You're not in trouble with the cops, are you?"

"Oh, thank god, no! But I need a favor, and I could only think of you."

"Go ahead."

Cáel went on to relate the happenings of the night of Michael's death, her injury, and her doubts about the whole story. The detective patiently heard her out, asking questions here and there. Finally, Cáel came to the reason of her phone call.

"I need to go over the case evidence and paperwork. I know I can gain access to them through the official channels, but it would simply take too long."

"So, let me get this straight. You're asking me to give you the stuff on the sly? You do know it's going to put my job on the line."

"I understand that, Detective, but it's a matter of life and death! You have to help me! I promise you I will return it all to you in twenty-four hours."

"Okay, I know a guy in archives who owes me. I'll see what I can do... why don't you stop by my office in the evening, say, around six o'clock?"

Cáel noted down the address and thanked him profusely.

***

It had been an agonizing wait for the evening through the day, and Cáel felt as though the hours stretched on and on for miles. She watched reruns on the television, cleaned, and dusted her whole house and then watched reruns again with the TV remote in her hands, sifting from channel to channel.

At five o'clock in the evening, she could stand it no more. She locked her front door and glided down the stairs. She thought about driving out herself, but abandoned the idea because she realized she could not recall a lot of roads. She waved the taxi and reached the police headquarters in ten minutes. She went in and searched for the detective's office. After she had found the door with his name on it on the first floor, she hung around in the reception, killing time studying people until it was six sharp.

The offices were shutting down and the building emptying out as she made her way back to the first floor and knocked on the detective's door.

"Come in."

Cáel pushed the door open, and found herself

facing a tall, handsome police officer, the face familiar from her memories. She smiled and greeted him, eyeing his table for a bunch of papers.

"Sit, please," he said, as he reached below his chair, and straightening up, pulled out an ochre box.

"Here you are, Miss Darcie, but remember, I have to deposit this back in three days. Not a paper goes missing."

CHAPTER 28

It was dark by the time Cáel reached her door. She opened the lock and put the light on. A white envelope on the floor next to the door caught her eye instantly. She picked it up and opened it. It was an apology note from Christopher Bush. It said:

> Cáel, please forgive me. I think I've hurt your feelings. Please give me a chance to make things right and help you remember everything. I miss you, Chris.

She crumpled the note and threw it away. She realized that Christopher had been to her condo and she had probably just missed him. The hair at the back of her neck began to rise. She shook the eerie feeling away.

Placing the evidence box on her dining table, Cáel heated a glass of milk and grabbed some strawberries from the fridge. Kicking off her shoes, she made herself comfortable on a chair and opened the box. It was half-full with printed papers.

Cáel methodically went through every word on the sheets. They were recorded transcripts of description of the scene-of-crime and statements of various people associated with Russell, Chris, and Michael including their lawyers. It was lengthy reading and by the time she was through, it was past midnight.

And she hadn't found much.

The only thing she had found notice worthy was that Russell's story and Christopher's story did not match. Russell claimed that the gun went off only once, and in the upward direction, over everyone's heads, while Christopher asserted that the gun was fired arbitrarily, many times, and one bullet hit Michael.

Either one was telling the truth. One of them

was lying and Cáel had a fair idea of who it was.

If Russell was telling the truth, it meant something more happened at Christopher's house after Russell had run away into the darkness.

What? Who killed Michael?

Right now the only person who had an answer to that question was Christopher Bush. Cáel eyed the crumpled apology note by him, lying in one corner.

I was there too, that night. I have to remember!

Desperation started to creep into Cáel.

I need to talk to Chris. I have to continue playing his game. I have to pretend that I don't know much. This is the only solution.

***

The next day when Christopher called, Cáel let it ring a long time before she answered the phone.

"Cáel, hell, I th-thought you won't take my c-call again! Why are you punishing m-me like this?" Christopher blurted into the phone.

She took a deep breath before answering. "I'm sorry, Chris, I was mad at you... I shouldn't have been. Please, let's forget it."

"Yes, let's forget it, baby doll," Christopher had composed himself pretty fast, and had reverted back to his smooth voice.

"You've been there for me, and I trust you as my friend. It's just my hormones, I think. There're all over the place lately."

"Hey, let me make it up to you," the stammer was gone.

"I'd like that very much. In fact, take me out

to that chicken place you'd mentioned once. I'm craving chicken wings, extra spicy."

"You got it. Pick you up at seven."

***

Cáel had taken some care dressing up, choosing a dress that revealed her bosom, and deftly hid her growing tummy. Now knowing that she was a weakness for Christopher, she wanted to take full advantage of it and throw him off guard so that he would reveal something relevant.

Unfortunately, Christopher wasn't taking the bait. He was his normal, overly confident self, laughing and telling jokes as though everything was just peachy. Cáel hated every moment of the evening, and it was difficult to not shrug his hand off when he placed it on her shoulder or around her waist. Wanting the evening to end, she asked Christopher if he had an early morning.

"No worries, I can stay out late, I have an afternoon shift tomorrow. I don't have to be at work until midday and I'll be home till then. But I will call you as soon as I'm off work to see how you're doing."

"Sounds good to me. By the way, my cell phone is with me now. So, I'm contactable on that, too."

Christopher dropped Cáel in front of her condo. As he goodnight, he leaned slightly forward, as if wanting to kiss her. She quickly turned away and said a breezy goodnight as she yanked the car door open. Chris drove away, looking rather crestfallen.

As if suffering his company isn't enough, he actually thought I'd kiss him; Cáel grimaced incredulously while unlocking her door. Letting herself in, she dumped her bag on the floor, and lay back on the sofa.

What a wasted evening. Nothing came out

of it. How many such evenings do I have to suffer, before I can remember something?

The same questions started plaguing her again. How did Michael die, who killed Michael? Was it Russell who accidentally killed Mike or... it's time to take a drive to the crime scene. Chris won't be home in the afternoon tomorrow. This is my chance to end this torture, once and for all.

Cáel then realized she didn't quite remember where Christopher lived. She wondered where she could find out. She did not want to ask Amanda, for she would suspect what she was planning on and freak out.

Then she remembered the ochre box of evidence. It was still sitting on her table. The address of the crime scene was in it. She went over and opened it, looking for a copy of the form on which the case had been registered officially. She found it right at the bottom and picked it up.

CHAPTER 29

The next afternoon, Cáel was driving her own car for the first time since her accident. She had decided to use it to get to Christopher's house for greater mobility. As she drove, she found that she didn't really have to consult her GPS, she was cruising toward Christopher's house on dead reckoning. It was a route she had driven many times, and she had driven it on the evening of the tenth of January too.

She drove to Whitney and reached the lane on which Christopher lived. As she saw the house, she was consumed by a clear flashback of the scene outside that house that fateful night.

She was on a stretcher... police sirens were ravaging her ears, and then she had seen Michael right next to her in the ambulance. Someone was zipping him up in the body bag.

Water streamed down Cáel's eyes profusely at

the remembrance. She had to stop driving to get a hold of herself. Her head slumped to the steering wheel, her heart threatening to implode. The grief of the morbid scene made her almost gag.

She drank a swig of water from her bottle on the adjacent seat. She breathed deep and long, and told herself, I can do this, Mike, my love, give me the strength to do this, to remember what had happened and bring justice to the table for you. I can't go on without knowing what happened and how it happened.

Cáel slowly moved the car forward. She parked her car around the bend, close to Christopher's house. From that vantage point, she could see Christopher's garage, and the patio. A wooden fence surrounded the property.

Cáel got out of the car and stared at the house, reliving the same vision of a few minutes ago, again. A shudder shook her whole body.

She crossed the distance and trooped to the fence, finding the gate which led into Christopher's backyard. It was latched, but not locked. She bent over it and reached in to open the latch.

She had entered Christopher's premises and walked to the front of the dwelling, taking in the front veranda and driveway. She walked up the steps and tried the door tentatively. It was locked.

Cáel made her way through the overgrown grass to the back, and tried opening the old wooden door built into the back wall of the kitchen. It was locked. She walked back the same way, trying every single window she crossed. They were all locked. She sighed in exasperation and then she saw sliding doors of the living room. They were closed. She tried sliding one open.

It opened and Cáel was inside.

The room was illuminated softly by the afternoon light. The whole house was silent.

Cáel felt a great sense of familiarity in the house, like she had been there many times, although after her accident, this was the first time. Memories started coming rapidly in her consciousness. She remembered shopping for groceries with Christopher and helping him stack them up in his kitchen shelves. She remembered cooking for Christopher... and Michael. It was a memory from happier times.

She shook her head in sadness. The sight of the black leather sofas in the living room nudged her into a strong reminiscence and she was taken back in time to the night of January tenth.

She was sitting with Michael on one of the couches, while Chris was hovering around. She and Michael had gone together to sign up for the prenatal classes. Cáel was confused about Michael's interest in the baby and it had thrown her off. Now, she had come over to have an adult conversation with Michael.

They were looking at each other and neither was talking. Christopher announced that he was going for a quick shower. In the background, Christopher's roommate, Russell, was loudly talking on the phone in his room, his words laced with swear words.

Cáel and Michael both started talking together and stopped abruptly to let the other speak. Cáel laughed softly. Then she was serious.

"How's Lily?"

"What? What do you know about Lily?"

Michael had started to frown, he was taken aback at Lily's name and wasn't looking happy.

"I know you're dating."

"I'm not...we are not dating. Our parents tried

it, but I'm not into her. I'm into you, Cáel."

Michael had looked into her eyes and Cáel's heart had somersaulted, but there was no way she was going to let him know that.

"That's the beauty of hindsight, isn't it?"

"Cáel, baby, I panicked. This was out of the blue. Seeing you again a few days ago made me realize how much I missed having you in my life."

Michael had let out a frustrated sigh and searched Cáel's face intently. Just then Russell's angry voice had filled the house, making Cáel jump out of her skin.

"What's going on?"

She had asked Christopher, who was out from his bath, and hanging around between in the kitchen and the living room.

"I don't know... he's in an argument with someone over a girl, I think."

Just then a door inside had slammed hard, and a livid Russell came marching out. He was headed toward the main door, a silver-gray gun in his hand.

"Hey!" Christopher had cried out and rushed after Russell, who had slipped out the door. Michael had instantly shot up from the sofa and gone after them.

Cáel sat bewildered. She could hear voices and a scuffle going on outside. Suddenly a deafening gunshot rang loudly through the still air, jerking her to her feet.

"Michael!" Cáel screamed as she ran toward the door leading out. Her foot got stuck within a stray string at the edge of the carpet and she violently stumbled to the floor, her head hitting the edge of the adjacent sofa with full force of the momentum of her dash to the door.

Cáel was dazed and the room swam in and out of her vision which was red with blood from her temple.

"Michael!"

She had tried calling out, but her voice was nothing more than a faint whisper.

***

Cáel heard a car engine outside, and she slipped into the present from her flashback.

She blinked once, twice, trying to understand what was happening when it hit her that Christopher was back.

She broke out of her trance, rushed to the nearest window and peered across the patio. What she saw froze her. It was Christopher! And he was walking toward the patio from his garage.

With record speed she sprinted toward the backdoor in the kitchen and let herself out, just as she heard the front door open noisily.

She tore through the garden on the side and skipped over the hedge, into the safety of her car.

"Holy freakin' hell!" She exclaimed as she fumbled for the keys. "That was too close!"

At last she shoved the key in the ignition and the car's engine came to life. She backed out carefully from the side lane and reversed into the main lane, slowly driving past Christopher's front gate.

Meanwhile, Christopher stepped out into his patio and was lighting a cigarette as he saw a blue sedan pass by his gate. The sticker on the back said, "Catch me if you can."

He recognized it right away and gazed at it, while unhurriedly blowing smoke out of his lips, until it disappeared from view.

Then he sauntered in and found his cell phone.

***

When Cáel was halfway to her home, her cell phone beeped a message. She picked it up and saw Christopher's name. She stopped her car and, with trembling fingers, she opened the message. The text read:

"Why are you in my neighborhood?"

CHAPTER 30

Damn, he has seen me!

Sweat broke out of Cáel's temples as she stared at Christopher's message. Now that he knew, Cáel decided to stop the games. Gathering courage, she replied to the text:

> "I am going to get you and when I do, the whole world will know the truth about you."

Tossing her phone on the back seat, she drove straight through the traffic to Black Mountain, striving to calm her nerves and catch her breath at the same time. Her phone started ringing as she got out of her car. It was Christopher.

With rising panic, Cáel went up to her condo. She locked and double-locked her door, and immediately called Detective Arnold. The phone rang at the other end. Answer, Answer!

"Detective, it's Cáel Darcie!" She nearly screamed into the phone when he picked up the receiver.

Cáel explained the scene to the detective as precisely as she could.

"I'll come over. Lock all the doors and wait."

As soon as she hung up, the telephone started to ring again. It was Christopher calling. She gawked at the ringing phone until it stopped. Then a message tone beeped on her cell, making her turn wildly toward it. She grabbed the cell phone and opened the message. It was from Christopher.

"I know you're there and I am coming to make things right."

Cáel started to pace around her room like a crazy woman. Her panic was now giving way to extreme anger. Adrenaline pumped through her veins, making her head throb in alertness, and her ears sensitive to every little sound. She ran to the kitchen and grabbed a large sharp knife. Gripping it tightly with both her hands, she settled down on the floor next to the door, breathing rapidly. She studied the knife, feeling its weight, and unexpectedly, she slipped into a clear and sharp memory of the rest of the evening of the tenth of January.

Cáel was dazed and the room swam in and out of her vision which was red with blood from her temple.

"Michael!"

She tried calling out, but her voice was a faint whisper.

For a few minutes, she had been unconscious, but floated back to consciousness when she heard voices outside. It was Michael's voice. Thank God, he's okay, she had thought.

She could hear their footsteps coming closer.

She tried opening her eyes but her eyelids felt like a bag of bricks.

"Cáel! ....Oh my God!"

Suddenly Michael was by her side, trying to pick her up.

"Chris, help me out, she's out cold! Cáel, Cáel... Sweetheart! Call 911, Chris!"

"Not before I get rid to you, you slime bag!"

Cáel could hear the entire conversation in her stupor. She tried speaking, but her lips didn't move.

"Leave her right where she is!" It was Chris.

"Hey! What's gotten into you, man? Why are you pointing that gun at me?"

"Because I want you to d-die!"

Chris was shouting, his stammer was now well-pronounced.

"I h- hate you. You've taken every prize, every laurel away from m-me, and you call yourself my f-friend?"

"What the hell are you talking about?"

Michael had left Cáel on the floor and was backing away slowly.

"W-what the hell am I t-talking about? The 'best-in-combat' trophy, for starters. That was supposed to be mine. You got it. You had the friends, the girls, the attention. 'Mr. Boy-wonder' you… I was always in your shadow, always looking for scraps from you. And then you started doing her?? She was supposed to be mine! I saw her first!"

Christopher had lowered his voice and was laughing maniacally.

"You're insane!"

A shot rang out.

No, No! Cáel howled inside her head. She heard Michael slumping and falling on the floor.

No! No! You won't get away with this!

***

Tears ran down Cáel's cheeks as she came back to real time.

He killed Mike. Christopher Bush killed him in cold blood!"
Cáel's phone rang out loudly in the room right then. She went over and glanced at the caller ID. It was Christopher. She picked up the receiver carefully, the hair at the back of her neck rising.

"Give yourself up, Christopher." There was

steel in Cáel's voice.

"Doll," Chris drawled in a thin quiet voice that made her spine chill, "What have you been up to?" Chris asked her in a strange sing-song tone.

"I know what you did, Chris. I remember every single thing!"

"Remember? You were out cold, woman. What are you threatening me with?"

"You thought I was out cold. But I could hear everything that happened. I heard your exchange. I heard you throw accusations on him which were just a figment of your demented imagination. Then you shot Mike. You dragged Mike out and made it look like he was shot by Russell. Russell had fired his gun in the scuffle, but he didn't shoot anyone. You shot Michael in cold blood out of jealousy!"

"I should've killed you too, along with that

son-of-a-bitch. So, now you know. Big deal! Who's going to believe you?"

"Christopher, give yourself up! You've committed a crime!"

A low laugh resounded from the phone.

"I would love to finish you off too, my doll. My lust for you got the better of me the last time. I thought you won't remember any of it and we would walk together into the sunset. I had a plan to get rid of that child of yours too! Alas! It's not to be."

"Chris, give yourself up, or I'll find you, I swear on Mike's baby, I will find you and make you pay for what you did to Mike!"

"A soldier never gives himself up, Cáel. And he never leaves a job unfinished. We'll meet soon. Goodbye for now!"

A click on the other end finished the call.

About the Author

Born in Haiti and raised in Florida, Naghilia Desravines has risen from overwhelming poverty. Having battled social evils such as abuse and racism throughout her childhood, Desravines has striven to become a dynamic, brilliantly creative, businesswoman.

She was raised by a grandfather who instilled in her strong family values, empathy, and a respect for relationships. As a young uneducated child, Desravines understood the importance of education to help break the endless cycle of poverty, and doggedly pursued her Master's degree in psychology, making her place in the world as a creative entrepreneur and author.

Cold Hearted is her first novel.

Coming Soon
Cold Hearted II

Photo by Kenji Kita

Printed by Libri Plureos GmbH in Hamburg, Germany